THE TEFLON QUEEN 6

NO MERCY

PROLOGUE

"LONDON"

Ashley zoomed from lane to lane on the highway like a mad woman. The engine on the Porsche she drove roared loudly as Ashley quickly swerved around a U-Haul truck avoiding a major accident. She glanced down at the speedometer that read 110 mph. "Hey don't lose him!" Troy's voice sounded off loudly through her earpiece.

"I got him!" Ashley replied in a cool tone as she kept her eye on the man on the motorcycle. The rider on the motorcycle was a well know British spy slash assassin that went by the name, Mad Max. Mad Max weaved two lanes over to his right he had no clue who was chasing behind him in the Porsche but what he did know was whoever was behind the wheel had to be a professional. The back of Mad Max's shirt flapped violently in the wind as the motorcycle reached the speed of 153 mph. Without warning, Mad Max dipped his body down to the right and quickly exited off the ramp in an attempt to lose the Porsche. Mad Max zoomed down the ramp and quickly merged on to another highway. He looked over his shoulder and through the visor on his helmet, he saw the Porsche still tailing him. Attached to Mad Max's back was a book bag with a laptop inside. But this wasn't any ole laptop; this laptop had some valuable information on it, information that could put the entire country in danger. The information on the laptop was so valuable that Mad Max was willing to risk his own life to obtain the information on that computer. Mad Max held on to the handle bars with one hand and pulled a 9mm from the holster on his waist with the other hand and sent four shots through Ashley's windshield.

Ashley ducked down as the bullets from Mad Max's gun shattered the Porsche's windshield making it difficult for her to see. "Ashley, we can't let him get away with that laptop!" Troy's voice snapped through her earpiece. Troy sat in the back of a van watching the entire thing play out on several computer monitors. The driver of the van did his best to try and keep up with Ashley and the driver of the motorcycle but he was having a hard time keeping up with their speed. "Ashley, there's a road block coming up ahead we just have to hope he doesn't get off this exit coming up," Ashley heard Troy's voice loud and clear through her earpiece.

Mad Max noticed the roadblock up ahead and quickly got off on the next exit. He knew he couldn't afford to get jammed up especially not with the content that rested in his book bag. Mad Max looked over his shoulder and fired a couple of shots into the windshield of several commuters causing a semi road.

"Shit!" Ashley stomped down hard on her brakes to avoid running into the back of a station wagon. She quickly threw the gear in reverse, backed up a bit, threw the gear back in drive, and swerved around the pile up. "Do you have eyes on the target?"

"Yes," Troy replied quickly. "He just made a right at the second light up ahead." Ashley gunned the engine determined not to lose her target. She made a right at the light and spotted the motorcycle flying down the street. Mad Max bunny hopped up onto the sidewalk forcing pedestrians to damn near kill themselves to avoid getting ran over.

"He just jumped the curb!" Troy's voice snapped through Ashley's earpiece. "There's a train station up ahead I think that's where he's headed."

Mad Max reached the tube and rode his bike down the first flight of stairs he had no care what so ever for innocent people anyone in his way was getting ran over no if, and, or buts about it. When Mad Max reached the bottom landing, he quickly let his bike crash to the ground as he removed his helmet and proceeded to blend in with the extremely large crowd.

Ashley's Porsche came to a skidding stop In front of the tube. She quickly dashed out the vehicle and made her way down the steps. When Ashley reached the bottom landing, she spotted the motorcycle laying on the ground next to a motorcycle helmet. "He's on foot," Ashley said into her earpiece, as she wasted no time walking into the large crowd looking for her target. "Troy I'm going to need some eyes down here!"

"I'm working on it," Troy replied as he searched each and every surveillance camera. There were so many people in the station that he knew it would be damn near impossible to spot the masked man with the book bag.

Ashley bumped and pushed her way through the large crowd of people as her eyes scanned from left to right in search for her target. "Troy, any luck?"

"Sorry Ashley but its rush hour on the tube," Troy explained while still searching each and every camera for the target. Troy's eyes moved all around the several monitors until he spotted the target. "Hey I found him! He just entered the men's room on the west wing."

"Copy," Ashley replied and headed towards the west wing.

"Please be extremely careful this man looks to be very dangerous," Troy pointed out.

"Dangerous is my middle name," Ashley said as she kept her hand down in her purse with her finger wrapped around the trigger of a pearl handled .380 with a silencer attached to the barrel. Ashely moved through the crowd like a ghost there was a lot at stake and she couldn't afford to lose that laptop by any means.

***

Mad Max entered the restroom and spotted a man wearing a hoodie at the sink washing his hands. Without warning, he grabbed the man by the back of his neck and violently rammed his head into the mirror shattering it in a million pieces. Mad Max quickly swept the man's feet from under him then roughly removed the hoodie from off the man's back. Mad Max slipped the hoodie over his head and pulled the strings down tight in an attempt to hide his identity. Mad Max exited the men's room and quickly blended back in with the crowd. He knew that there were people after him and what was in his book bag and he refused to get captured and if he did, he sure as hell wasn't going down without a fight.

***

"I'm approaching the men's room now," Ashley said as she pushed the restroom door open with cation. She stepped inside and immediately spotted a man lying on the floor, his face covered in blood. "What happened?" Ashley asked.

"Some asshole came in here and robbed me for my hoodie," the man explained with blood running down his fingers.

"What color was the hoodie?"

"Huh?"

"What color was the hoodie?" Ashley screamed in the man's face.

"Navy blue," the man replied with a scared look on his face.

Ashley quickly rushed out of the men's room. "The target is on the move and he's wearing a navy blue hoodie," she told Troy as she power walked through out the station in search of anyone wearing a navy blue hoodie. Troy searched his monitors and a minute and a half later, he spotted their target.

"I got him!" Troy said. He's about two hundred and fifty feet away standing on the platform. "Hurry because I think a train should be arriving soon."

Ashley hurried down the escalator then stepped on the platform snaking her way through the large crowd of people who stood on the platform awaiting their train's arrival. After a minor search, Ashley spotted a figure with his back to her wearing a navy blue hoodie. Ashley pulled her .380 from her purse and let it hang freely by her side as she continued to inch her way towards her target.

***

Mad Max stood on the platform with his hands buried in the pocket of his hoodie. In his right hand, he held a tight grip on his P-90 handgun. His mind was already made up either he was leaving with the laptop or he wasn't leaving alive his options were pretty simple. Mad Max felt the rumble of a train approaching.

Just as he was about to get his hopes up, Mad Max heard a females voice yell, "freeze!" coming from behind him.

Mad Max slowly raised his hands in surrender then began screaming. "Help! Help! She's trying to rob me! Help!"

Before Ashley realized what was going on, she was roughly tackled down to the pavement by two strong pedestrians who called themselves doing a good deed. Once Mad Max saw Ashley get tackled down to the floor, he took off in a sprint in the opposite direction.

"Get the hell off of me!" Ashley yelled, as she was finally able to wrestle her way back to her feet. She was about to go chase after her target but stopped in mid-stride when she saw one of the pedestrians holding her at gunpoint with her own gun.

"Shit!"

***

Mad Max sprinted full speed through the train station. Getting caught wasn't an option. He pushed and shoved going and coming passengers out of his way. Mad Max turned the corner and ran dead smack into a police officer.

"Whoa!" the officer said in a stern tone. "Where you rushing too?"

"Sorry officer, I was just trying to catch my girlfriend before she left," Mad Max lied in an innocent tone. From the outside, looking in one would never know that he was one of the most dangerous men in the world.

"Let me see some I.D."

"Officer, I really need to get going," Mad Max tried to brush past the officer but a firm hand to the chest stopped his momentum.

"You're not going anywhere until I see some form of I.D." the officer said as his hand fell down to his side next to his holster. Mad Max slowly reached in his back pocket and removed his wallet; he removed his I.D., and held it out so the officer could see it. Once Mad Max was sure that the officer's eyes were glued to the I.D., his hand shot out and chopped the officer in the throat. Before the officer could recover, Mad Max snatched the .357 from the officer's holster and fired two shots to the officer's face. Before the officer's body could even hit the floor, Mad Max was already sprinting towards the other said of the station. Mad Max sprinted through the station when he heard two gunshots ring out.

Without warning, Mad Max grabbed the closet woman next to him and used her as a human shield. To Mad Max's left he spotted another officer in a low crouch aiming his gun in his direction the only thing that stopped the officer from pulling the trigger were all of the innocent people running and screaming for their lives. Mad Max fired two shots in the officer's direction. When he saw the officer crumble down to the floor, he roughly shoved the woman he was using as a shield to the floor and made his way down the escalator. As Mad Max rode down the escalator, he noticed an officer at the bottom of the escalator talking on his walkie-talkie. When Mad Max made it to the bottom of the escalator he turned and slapped the officer across the face with the .357 the impact from the blow dropped the officer. Mad Max stood over the officer and pistol-whipped him until his face was no longer recognizable. Mad Max then quickly disappeared off into the crowd.

CHAPTER 1

"BIG TROUBLE"

The next day, Ashley stepped foot in headquarters and immediately she could feel the energy in the entire building was down. Deep down inside, Ashley felt as if everything was her fault since she was the one who allowed Mad Max to escape. Ashley walked down the hall towards Captain Spiller's office. The closer she got to Captain Spiller's office the louder she could hear his voice yelling from on the other side of the door. Ashley took a deep breath before knocking on the door.

Captain Spiller snatched the door open with a mean look on his face. "Get your ass in here right now!" He scowled. Ashley stepped inside the office and saw Troy and a few other agents that she recognized sitting at the table.

"Now maybe you can help me understand how you let a terrorist get away with one of our agent laptops?" Captain Spiller huffed.

"I had him until a few Good Samaritan's tackled me to the ground," Ashley pointed out.

"How in the hell did you all allow a British spy to walk into a secure building and leave out with a laptop!" Captain Spiller barked. "Do any of you even know what was on that laptop?" He looked around the room. Everyone remained silent. "He hacked into one of the main systems and downloaded the name of every special agent onto that laptop."

"Shit!" Ashley mumbled. With that type of information in the wrong hands, things could turn bad real quick.

"Our target goes by the name, Mad Max. He's well trained and is as good they come," Captain Spiller explained. "We don't know who Mad Max is working for as of yet but what we do know is that no agent is safe," Captain Spiller paused for a second. "Mad Max was last seen in Las Vegas where three special agents mysteriously ended up dead. My guest is he's going to go down the entire list until every last agent is dead and gone," Captain Spiller turned his focus on Ashley. "We can't allow that to happen so we are going to have to catch him and catch him quickly."

"Where was he last seen?" Troy asked.

"Washington D.C." Captain Spiller replied.

"How many agents do we have out there?" Troy asked.

"Too many!" was Captain Spiller's response. "I need y'all to find Mad Max and put him down before any other agents turn up missing."

"Don't worry, we'll find him," Ashley assured the captain.

"Hey also I need you to reach out to Angela and let her know about this situation," Captain Spiller said.

"Angela has been out of the game for a year now," Ashley replied. "You don't think Mad Max would come for her would you?"

"I doubt it," Captain Spiller said quickly. "But her name is still on that list so just give her the heads up," Captain Spiller said then exited his office. Ashley knew that if they didn't find Mad Max soon things were sure to spiral out of control especially once the media caught wind of these agents mysteriously coming up dead.

"We have to find this asshole before another agent comes up missing," Troy said with a stressful look on his face.

CHAPTER 2

"WASHINGTON, D.C."

Mad Max sat staked out in an old school brown station wagon. Across the street to his left was a nice single family home. On Mad Max's lap sat a picture and file of the next agent that was on his hit list. The agent went by the name Robert Banks and was said to be one of the best agents out there. Mad Max watched the house closely and as soon as he saw the light from the main bedroom go off, he made his move. Mad Max stepped out of his vehicle and walked swiftly towards the house. He pulled a

.380 from the holster on his hip and screwed a silencer onto the barrel. Mad Max reached the front door, removed a small box from his back pocket, and placed it against the lock on the door. Ten seconds later, the small box made a soft beeping sound and the lock mysteriously opened. Mad Max let himself inside and quietly closed the door behind him. The entire house was dark so Mad Max had to be very careful not to bump into something that would alert his target. Mad Max eased his way through the house and stepped on a rubber duck that was left on the floor by one of Agent Banks' kids. The rubber duck squealed loudly under the pressure of Mad Max's foot.

***

Agent Robert Banks laid in bed with his wife Stacey watching CNN when they heard a noise coming from downstairs. Agent Banks sat up and looked at his wife. "You heard that?"

Stacey nodded with a scared look on her face. Agent Banks got out of bed, grabbed his 9mm off the nightstand, and made his way downstairs. Agent Banks eased his way down the steps making sure not to make the slightest bit of noise. He knew his way around his house well and was able to maneuver in the dark. Agent Banks stepped in the kitchen and instantly got a bad feeling as if he was being watched. Agent Banks noticed something move through the reflection from the kitchen window and ducked down just in time as a silent bullet shattered the window. Agent Banks accidentally dropped his weapon in the process. Having no other options, he rushed the gunman and grabbed the arm of the gunman, held the gun in, and raised it towards the ceiling as the two men struggled for possession of the firearm. The gun discharged several times in Mad Max's hands as he and Agent Banks went crashing back into the dining room table. Mad Max delivered two knees to Agent Banks' stomach as the gun hit the floor. He then landed a sharp elbow to the side of Agent Banks' face that opened up a cut right above the special agent's eye. Agent Banks quickly dropped down to the floor and reached for the gun. Mad Max kicked the gun out of arms reach as he raised his foot and stomped Agent Banks' head into the floor. Mad Max roughly snatched the agent back up to his feet and unloaded a six-punch combo to the agent's already bloody face. Agent Banks tried to fight back but his skills were nowhere near on the level as Mad Max. Mad Max easily weaved and dodged the agent's punches. Mad Max faked like he was about to throw a jab then landed a swift kick to the side of Agent Banks that took him off his feet. Mad Max then grabbed a knife from off the knife rack and stabbed Agent Banks repeatedly in his face. Once Mad Max was sure that Agent Banks was dead, he forcefully jammed the knife into agent Banks' eye socket and slowly stood to his feet. He pulled his back up .22 from the small of his back and headed upstairs to finish off agent Banks' wife.

***

"There's over five hundred agent here in D.C.," Troy pointed out as him and Ashley cruised through the D.C. streets. "Where do we start?"

"I don't know," Ashley replied as she looked at a folder that held every agent in D.C. name and address. She knew tracking down this spy slash assassin know as Mad Max was going to be harder than she expected. From the little run-in she had with Mad Max in London, Ashley knew that he was going to be a problem. "Captain said an alert went out to all of the agent's notifying them what was going on so they should be on point if any trouble comes there way," Ashley said as she felt her cell phone vibrating in her pocket. She looked at her iPhone and saw

Captain Spiller's name flashing across the screen. "What up, Captain?" she answered.

"A silent alarm just went off at one of our agent's home out in South East D.C. I have a bad feeling that our friend Mad Max is there," Captain Spiller explained. "I just texted you and Troy the address. How far away from there are y'all?"

"How far are we from that address?" Ashley asked as she watched Troy quickly type the address into the GPS.

"Eight minutes away, but I can get us there in four!" Troy said as he stomped down on the brakes and hit an illegal U-turn.

"We'll be there in four minutes, Captain!"

"Make it three!" Captain Spiller yelled then ended the call.

***

Mad Max made his way upstairs and entered the master bedroom with caution. He looked around the room and saw light coming from underneath the door in the bathroom. He quickly walked over to the door and grabbed the doorknob only to find out that it was locked. Without warning Mad Max took a step back and came forward and landed a strong kick on the bathroom door. He kicked the door repeated until he felt the door finally beginning to give.

On the other side of the door, Stacey stood in the tub with tears running down her face as she held a .357 with a shaky two-handed grip. "The police are on the way!" She yelled hoping to scare the gunman off.

Bang! Bang! Bang!

The kicks became louder and louder with each passing second.

Mad Max took another step back and landed a sidekick that sent the door flying off the hinges. Just as he went to enter the bathroom, he heard the loud blast from a big handgun. Mad Max ducked just in time as a big chunk of the wall came crumbling down on his head. Mad Max kept his body out of harm's way, stuck his arm in the bathroom, and fired seven shots in rapid succession until he heard a low grunt followed by the sound of Stacey's body collapsing down to the floor. Mad Max then stepped in the bathroom and fired two more shots in the woman's head for extra emphasis. Mad Max exited the bedroom when he heard the sound of someone entering the house downstairs.

Officer Lowry, a uniform officer who had only been on the force for two month, was the first to arrive at the scene of the crime. Officer Lowry entered the house with caution, immediately removed his flashlight from his belt, and let the light guide him through the property. "Police, anyone home!" he yelled as he moved through the house. As Officer Lowry continued on throughout the house, he came across a dead body lying in the middle of the floor. He quickly reached for his holster and panicked when he realized that his service pistol was no longer in his holster. Officer Lowry heard a slight noise and quickly spun to his left only to find himself looking down the barrel of his own .357.

Officer Lowry threw his hands up in surrender and began to beg for his life. "I have a wife and a newborn baby at..."

Mad Max shot the officer in the face at pointblank range not allowing him to finish his dialogue. Mad Max heard another car come to a screeching stop in front of the house, he peeked through the blinds and spotted the same woman he had bumped into out in London exited the vehicle. Mad Max quickly stepped over the dead bodies and quietly exited throughout the back door.

***

Ashley pulled her Five-Seven pistol from her holster as she entered the house with Troy close on her heels. Immediately she spotted two bodies ahead of her. When Ashley reached the first body, she slowly kneeled down and checked for a pulse. She looked up at Troy and shook her head no. Troy nodded straight ahead. When Ashley looked up, she saw the back door was left open. "Damn!" she cursed.

Thirty minutes later, Agent Banks' house was filled with cops and other agents.

Captain Spiller stepped in the house with a pissed off look on his face as usual. "Please tell me Mad Max is laying in the back yard with a bullet in his head."

"Sorry Captain, we got here like three minutes late," Ashley said. She knew they had missed a big chance at catching their target and now their mission would only become more difficult.

"He could be anywhere by now!" Captain Spiller barked. "And with so many agents in this city it'll be damn near impossible to predict where he'll be striking next."

"The only thing we can do is wait and see if his pattern begins to get predictable," Troy said. "That or hope and pray he runs across the wrong agent."

"Have you spoke to Angela yet?" Captain Spiller turned his gaze on Ashley.

"I called her but she didn't answer."

"I need you to personally go pay Angela a visit and let her know exactly what's going on," Captain Spiller said. "And make sure that she knows her name is on that list."

"I'll do it first thing in the morning," Ashley replied.

Later on that night, Ashley entered her hotel room and flopped down on the bed. She was beginning to get frustrated. It was taking so long for them to find and locate Mad Max that she was starting to lose faith in if they would be able to find their target before it was too late. Ashley pulled out her phone and dialed Angela's number. The phone rang out before reaching the voicemail. She tossed her phone down on the bed and stared up at the ceiling until she finally drifted off to sleep.

CHAPTER 3

"A FRESH START"

Angela stood in her basement shadow boxing with an intense look on her face. She may have been out of the game but she still kept herself in tiptop shape. Angela threw a quick left, right hook, followed by a swift upper cut when she heard someone enter the basement.

"Mommy!" Little Angela ran in the basement and hugged Angela's leg tightly.

"What are you doing awake?" Angela smiled as she picked little Angela up.

"I wanted to watch cartoons, Mommy!" Little Angela squealed loudly.

Angela smiled when she looked up and saw David enter the basement.

"Sorry baby I know you were down here working out," David said as he kissed Angela on the lips and took Little Angela from Angela's arms. "She's fast for a three year old." David smiled. "Finish your workout my queen, breakfast will be ready in about thirty minutes," he said as he and Little Angela exited the basement. All Angela could do was smile. She had been dating David for the past year and their relationship was great. David was a good man and treated Angela like a queen. Three months ago, Angela and David decided to adopt a three-year-old baby. David wanted to have a baby but Angela wasn't ready for all that, so the two decided to adopt instead. Angela was loving her new life and the best thing about it was David knew nothing about her past or what she used to do for a living. For once, Angela was able to live a normal life and enjoy simple things like birthdays, go on vacation, and not have to always look over her shoulder ever two seconds or dodge bullets. When David asked Angela what she did for a living she simply told him that she no longer had to work because she had gotten hit with a few stray bullets from a police officer who was having a shootout with a criminal. Angela made up that story because she knew David would have questions when he saw the scars from the bullets on her body. She hated that she had to lie to David but it was for his own good. The less he knew the better it was for him.

Angela finished her workout and headed straight for the shower where she did all her thinking and meditating. Angela stepped out of the shower, dried off, threw on a pair of black stretch pants, a black wife beater, and headed downstairs barefoot to join her family at the breakfast table.

Angela made it downstairs and found David and little Angela sitting down at the table waiting for her to join them.

"Come on mommy," little Angela said. "We were waiting for you to come downstairs so we could pray and eat," she said innocently.

"You were working out pretty hard down in the basement," David smiled. "Trying to keep it nice and tight for me?"

Angela returned David's smile. "Of course," the three sat enjoying their meal when they heard a firm knock at the door. Immediately, Angela was on guard especially since they never had any visitors. Angela was living a low-key life and wanted to keep it that way.

"I'll get it honey," David pushed away from the table and headed towards the door. David opened the door without even looking through the peephole. "How are you doing? Can I help you?"

"Yes hi, my name is Ashley. I'm a close friend of Angela; is she home?" Ashley asked with a smile. "Sorry for just showing up unannounced like this."

"No problem come right on in," David stepped to the side so Ashley could enter. "Honey you have a visitor!" David called out as him and Ashley entered the kitchen.

Angela's eyes lit up when she saw Ashley standing in her kitchen. She was happy to see Ashley but she also knew that if she was standing in her kitchen that meant something serious had to be going on. Angela stood up and hugged Ashley tightly. Even though Angela knew some drama was sure to come behind this visit, she was happy to see Ashley was still alive and in one piece.

"Mommy who's that?" Little Angie pointed with sticky fingers.

"This here is Ashley and she's like a sister to me," Angela smiled. "Excuse us while I go talk to Ashley in the other room."

"Sure baby go ahead," David said. "Me and Angie are going to tackle these dishes."

Angela led Ashley out front to the porch where the two helped themselves to a seat.

"So this is your new life huh?" Ashley looked around. "Looks very peaceful."

Angela nodded. "It's very peaceful out here and quiet."

"I didn't know you had a baby?" Ashley said. "She's beautiful."

"Thank you, we adopted her," Angela smiled. "She's my little angel." Angela looked out to the end of her driveway and noticed Ashley was driving a bulletproof BMW. "So let's cut to the chase what's going on and how bad is it?"

"Real bad," Ashley began. "A spy broke into headquarters out in London and downloaded the names and address of every special agent onto a laptop."

"And he escaped alive?" Angela asked with a raised brow. She knew that to pull something like that off was damn near impossible.

Ashley nodded her head. "Yes I ran into him on the tube but he managed to get away."

"He had to have some help," Angela said. "There's no way he was able to escape headquarters alive without some help on the inside."

"I was thinking the same thing," Ashley agreed.

"Okay so why are you here?" Angela asked with a raised brow.

"I know you're out the game but I wanted to come by and personally tell you to stay on point," Ashley paused for a second and handed Angela a folder. "An assassin that goes by the name Mad Max has been knocking off agents left and right."

"And let me guess, my name is on that list?" Angela opened the folder and examined the assassins face closely.

Ashley nodded. "All of our names are on that list."

"So you mean to tell me that this one assassin is taking out all of these agents one by one?"

Ashley nodded. "He's good, real good," she paused for a second. "It would great if you'd come out of retirement and help us catch this asshole."

"I'm done with all that," Angela replied quickly. "That part of my life is over with. I'm a mother now and I have a family to look after. I know you, Troy, and the rest of y'all can take out this assassin."

Ashley nodded. "I feel where you coming from," she dug down in her purse and pulled out a Five-Seven pistol and discreetly handed the handgun to Angela. "I'll feel better knowing you have this." Ashley stood to her feet and kissed Angela on the forehead. "I love you," Ashley said then turned and headed for her BMW. Angela watched as the BMW disappeared down the street, she then looked down to the pistol that rested in her hand. It had been a few years since the last time she held a gun in her hands.

Angela hoped and prayed that whatever drama was going on didn't make it to her neck of the woods and anywhere near her family. Angela heard the front door open and quickly stood up and stuck the gun down into the small of her back just as, lil Angie stepped out onto the porch.

"Mommy can we go to the park?"

"Yes, did you ask daddy to take you?" Angela ruffled lil Angie's hair and led her back inside.

"Yeah but he said he has to go to work," lil Angie said with a sad look on her face. "Can you take me mommy?"

"Of course I can baby, go get dressed," Angela smiled as she watched the baby run up the stairs towards her bedroom. Angela trotted upstairs, entered the master bedroom, and heard the shower running. She quickly walked over to her side of the bed while the coast was clear and hid the handgun under the mattress. Angela was trying to think positively, but she knew if Ashley came all this way to see her that the situation had to be worse than she had explained.

CHAPTER 4

"I'M HAPPY FOR YOU"

A shley sat at a red light behind the wheel of her BMW with a million and one thoughts running through her mind. Her getting a chance to see Angela made her happy. It had been a while since Ashley laid eyes on her mentor and just the sight of Angela brought back so many great memories. It was a little strange at first seeing Angela as a mom and housewife instead of the Teflon Queen, but Ashley had to admit Angela definitely seemed to be very happy and the entire atmosphere was so laid back and peaceful. As Ashley cruised down the street, she wondered if she could maybe see herself having a family in the future. She quickly shook that foolish notion out of her head. Right now Ashley needed to be on point. She pulled up to a five star hotel. Ashley stepped out the BMW and handed the keys to the valet employee who stood in front of the hotel. Ashley stepped foot inside the hotel and was ready to get down to business. She had gotten word that a man that fit the description of Mad Max had been seen in the hotel. "What floor?" Ashley boarded the elevator and quickly pressed the door close button repeatedly until finally the doors closed.

"He's on the eleventh floor," Troy's voice cackled through her earpiece. "He's in room 1724."

"Is he alone?"

"Yes he should be," Troy replied. "So what did Angela say when you saw her?"

"Didn't say much," Ashley replied as she removed her .380 from her purse and quickly attached the silencer to the barrel. "She seems really happy and at peace with her decision to leave all this behind and I'm happy for her."

"Well if she's happy then I'm happy," Troy countered.

"She's got a nice man and a beautiful daughter to live for now," Ashley stepped off the elevator and headed in the direction of room 1724. "Hit the cameras for a second while I do my thing."

Troy did as he was told and scrambled all of the security cameras with a press of a button on his laptop. Originally, Ashley was supposed to be waiting for backup to arrive, but taking in the severity of the situation Ashley figured it would be best to move in now before Mad Max decided to fall off the radar again.

Ashley shot the lock off the door and barged inside room 1724 with a strong two-handed grip on her weapon ready to shoot first and ask questions never. "Move and I'll blow your fucking head off!"

Ashley yelled in a stern tone. On the bed was a man and a woman who looked to be a prostitute in the middle of relieving one another's stress. The prostitute raised her hands high in the air. "Please don't shoot!" she yelled.

Ashley moved further inside the room, lowered her weapon, and breathed a sigh of relief when she realized the man on the bed wasn't Mad Max. "Shit we have a false alarm!" She stuck her gun back down into her purse and exited the room as if nothing happened.

"What happened?" Troy asked in a nervous tone. He was expecting to hear an abundance of gunshots.

"It wasn't him," Ashley said as she entered the staircase and headed back down to the lobby. Just as Ashley disappeared in the staircase, the elevator door slid open simultaneously and out stepped Mad Max. On this same exact floor was a female agent that went by the name, Agent Carter who resided in a room four doors down from where Ashley had just left. It just so happen that agent Carter was the next unlucky name on Mad Max's list.

Mad Max wore a long trench coat that hung down to his calves. The coat helped to hide the 12-gauge shotgun that hung from underneath his armpit. Mad Max walked to the end of the hall and stopped when he reached the room he was looking for, flipped his trench coat back, and pulled his shotgun from under his armpit. Attached to the end of the shotgun was a silencer. Mad Max raised the shotgun and blew the lock off the door.

***

Agent Carter stepped out of the bathroom covered in a towel. Laying on the bed in plain sight was a 9mm, a can of pepper spray, and an extra magazine. She had been fully warned about the British spy that's been taking agents out left and right and planned to be prepared if he ever came gunning for her. Agent Carter was a beautiful woman with blonde hair, blue eyes, with a nice athletic frame and build. Agent Carter applied lotion to her legs when she saw movement coming from the security camera she had set up outside of her door. Agent Cater took a closer look and saw a suspicious man walking down the hall heading towards her room. The thing that caused a red flag was the fact that the man was wearing a trench coat and looked as if he was trying to conceal something. Agent Carter quickly snatched her 9mm off the bed just as the lock on the room door exploded followed by the door being kicked in.

CHAPTER 5

"COME OUT AND PLAY"

M ad Max blew the lock off the door and quickly entered the room. On first glance, the room appeared to be empty but Mad Max knew better because he could smell the fresh scent of perfume lingering through the air that meant someone was inside. Mad Max cautiously eased his way through the suite being as quiet as possible when he saw Agent Carter spring from behind a wall and fire four shots in his direction. Mad Max quickly dropped, rolled, and quickly took cover behind a wall as two more bullets exploded right above his head.

Agent Carter fired off two more shots in Mad Max's direction then took off towards the bedroom and locked the door behind her. She quickly wiggled into a pair of stretch pant, threw a wife beater on, and headed straight for the window.

***

Mad Max waited a couple of seconds before he rounded the corner. He reached the bedroom and paused as he placed his ear close to the door listening for any sudden sounds that may give him an idea of what was going on, on the other side of the door. Five seconds later, Mad Max took a step back and kicked the room door open. The business end of his shotgun guiding him inside the room, which appeared to be empty at first sight. Mad Max walked over to the closet and blew two big holes through the door before opening it. He then made his way over to the bed and flipped the entire mattress off the bed, still no agent. Mad Max looked over to his left and notice the window open. He quickly walked over to the window and peeked out. Mad Max chuckled when he saw Agent Carter standing on the ledge about twelve feet away from him with a scared look on her face.

Agent Carter stood out on the ledge seventeen floors high in the air. She stared straight ahead in fear that if she looked down she would fall off the ledge and die a horrible death. She was cornered, nowhere left for her to go. Agent Carter closed her eyes and prayed for the best. After giving it some thought, maybe climbing out the window out onto the ledge wasn't such a good idea after all.

Mad Max positioned half of his body out the window and aimed his shotgun at Agent Carter's upper body. He cocked a round into the chamber and immediately Agent Carter's body flinched. Without warning Mad Max pulled the trigger and watched as the impact from the shotgun's pellets blew Agent Carter off the ledge like a strong gust of wind. Agent Carter's body floated through the air in what seemed like slow motion.

***

Ashley slid in the passenger seat of the white van that waited curbside for her; the look on her face said that she was pissed off. "Another wasted night."

"Well it was worth a try," Troy turned the key in the ignition making the engine on the van roar. "Don't worry we're going to catch this asshole."

"I'm not doubting that," Ashley said. "I just wonder how many more people have to die before we put this guy down." Ashley sat in the passenger seat thinking about all the families that lost their lives so far and wonder how many more would have to lose their lives before this sick game was all over. The longer it took for them to find and kill Mad Max meant more innocent people would likely get hurt and possibly killed and that wasn't sitting well with Ashley.

"Where we off to now?"

"Let's go grab something to eat," Ashley suggested as she stared blankly out the window in deep thought. Troy pulled away from the curb when something slammed down on the hood of the van with extreme force startling both him and Ashley. Ashley stepped out the car with a confused look on her face. She took a step back and saw a woman's body sprawled across the hood of the van. "Call an ambulance!" Ashley yelled as she ran back inside the hotel with her hand jammed down in her pocketbook, she held a firm grip on the handle of her firearm. Ashley had no idea where the body came from but she had a good idea. She stood at the elevator and paused for a second. "*If I was trying to escape a hotel I definitely wouldn't do it from the front door.*"

Ashley thought as she walked over to one of the hotel workers. "Excuse me where's the back exit?"

"Down that hall and around the corner," the worker pointed Ashley in the right direction. Ashley jogged down the hall, and when she turned the corner, she saw the exit to the back door slowly closing. Ashley pulled her 9mm from her purse, pushed her way through the back exit, and saw a man in a trench coat sprinting down the dark one-way street. "Suspect is on foot on a side street!" Ashley yelled into her earpiece as she took off after the man in the trench coat.

CHAPTER 6

"NOWHERE TO RUN"

Mad Max took off down the street and turned the corner just as a man on a motorcycle was riding by. Without warning, Mad Max stuck his arm out and violently clothes lined the rider off the bike. Mad Max quickly stood the bike up, hopped on, and dramatically made the back tire screech loudly as he took off like he was shot out of a cannon. Ashley rounded the corner and cursed loudly when she saw her target taking off down the street on a motorcycle. "Suspect is on a motorcycle headed north she said into her earpiece. Ashley ran out into the street and snatched a man who sat at a red light out the driver seat of his car. She hopped in the front seat, made an illegal U-turn, and proceeded after Mad Max. Ashley drove down the street like a mad man. "I need eyes on the target!" Ashley yelled into her earpiece.

"We lost him," Troy's voice came through Ashley's earpiece.

Ashley pulled back up in front of the hotel where Agent Carter had been shot out of a seventeenth floor window. She looked at all the news reporters and camera crews that flooded the entire block and all Ashley could do was shake her head. It seemed like no matter how hard she tried, Mad Max somehow continued to sneak through the cracks. Another agent was dead and the shooter was still out at large. Mad Max had the upper hand right now and was using his leverage wisely. All Ashley and the rest of the agents could do was play defense and wait for their name to pop up on Mad Max's list.

Captain Spiller pulled up in his usual foul mood. The more agents that ended up getting murdered made him and his entire team look bad. "Please tell me we have this asshole's whereabouts and we're just waiting for the right time to take him out."

"I wish that was the case," Ashley said in a low voice. "Captain, we have to find this animal and we have to find him soon before anymore agents end up dead."

"Ashley, I'm going to need you and Troy to hunt this Mad Max guy and kill him!" Captain Spiller barked. "Look at all this press out here," he paused to looked around at all the news crews and reporters that stood behind the yellow tape. "I need you and Troy to put an end to this once and for all I don't care how you did just get it done!"

Ashley watched as Captain Spiller stormed off to do an interview with one of the many reporters.

Ashley walked over to the side of the street where she saw Troy double-parked. Ashley slid in the passenger seat and banged her fist down on the dashboard out of frustration. "We have to catch this asshole!"

"I hate to say this but Mad Max has the upper hand right now," Troy said as he pulled away from the curb. "We have to somehow figure out a way to beat him to the punch and find out who his next victim is before he does."

"And how the hell are we supposed to do that?"

"We would basically have to set up a trap and hope Mad Max falls for the bait," Troy made it sound as if a task like that would be a piece of cake when in all reality getting a trained spy to fall into a trap was damn near impossible.

Troy pulled up, parked in front of a bar, and killed the engine. "I'm buying!"

Ashley sat at the bar, and for the first time in a long time, she had a smile on her face. Going out to the bar was just what she needed, her life had been all work for the last couple of years so hanging out in a bar felt like a vacation to her minus the sand and nice weather. "Thank you."

"For what?" Troy asked with a confused look on his face.

"Bringing me to this bar so I can take my mind off Mad Max. I really needed this," Ashley draped her arm around Troy's neck. "Sometimes I let this job get the best of me."

"We don't have a normal job," Troy sipped his drink. "Our job is to save the world."

Ashley chuckled. "Now I see why Angela decided to go and live a normal life," Ashley took another shot and almost slid off of her stool.

"Okay someone has had enough," Troy grabbed Ashley by the arm and led her back to the car. When the two made it outside, Ashley threw up all over the sidewalk, her shoes, and Troy's pants leg. Troy patted Ashley on the back lovingly. Troy had been working with Ashley and Angela for so long that they were no longer coworkers, they were more like family. Troy helped Ashley In the passenger seat. Tonight Troy and Ashley were able to toss a few drinks back but tomorrow it was back to live action.

CHAPTER 7

"OLD MEMORIES"

Angela stepped back inside her house from putting little Angie on the school bus and sat at the kitchen table. A lot of wild thoughts had been running through her mind after Ashley's pop-up visit. Angela wanted nothing else to do with the business or field she was in, but she also had a responsibility to protect her family by any means necessary. Angela had been watching the news and saw all the damage that the crazy assassin had been causing as well as all of the agents and their families who ended up dead. The thought of Angela's name being next on the assassin's hit list haunted her and sometimes kept her up at nights. Angela pushed away from the table and headed downstairs to the basement where she worked out for over an hour every day. Down in the basement was a treasure chest. Angela popped open the chest and looked inside. The other day while David was at work, Angela went out and purchased a shotgun, an M-1 rifle, and a .380 along with a silencer. Angela hated the fact that she had to hide things from David but she had to do what she had to do to protect her family. Every night, Angela prayed that the crazy assassin was either captured or killed. At least then, she'd know that her and her family would be safe. Angela grabbed the .380, attached the silencer to the barrel, and went out into the backyard and fired off a few rounds. She placed empty soda cans up and used them as targets. One by one Angela knocked down each soda can with ease. All of her skills were still in place; she just prayed she'd never have to use them again. Angela worked on her aim and accuracy for the next hour, took a shower, and then began to prepare dinner. Dave enjoyed home cooked meals so Angela took some cooking lessons so her skills in the kitchen could be just as good if not better than her skills out in the field. Angela stood over the stove when she felt a pair of hands gently grab her breast from behind. Angela quickly spun around; in the same motion, she landed an elbow to the side of the intruder's head. Angela got ready to finish the man off with a standing sidekick to the chin but stopped her leg in mid-air when she saw Dave holding the side of his head. "Oh my god, Dave!" Angela yelled. "I'm so sorry!"

"Baby relax it's just me," David said with his hand up in surrender. Angela helped Dave up to his feet.

"Sorry baby, I thought you were a burglar," Angela said as she grabbed an ice pack from out the freezer and pressed it against Dave's head. She felt bad for putting her hands on Dave but it was an honest mistake.

"Where the hell did you learn how to do a move like that?" Dave asked with a curious look on his face as he held the ice pack up to his head. The last time he'd seen a move like that was in a kung-fu movie.

"I took a karate class when I was younger," Angela lied. There was no way she could tell Dave that in her former life she was an assassin that happened to end up working for the C.I.A.

"Can you teach me that move?" Dave said playfully as he took a karate stance.

"You so silly," Angela nudged Dave playfully and headed down to the basement to make sure all of her weapons were put away and out of sight. Once that was done, Angela headed back upstairs to finish preparing dinner. Angela did her best to keep her past life a secret away from Dave and little Angie but with all the stuff that was going on the news, she had a bad feeling about this crazy assassin that was running around freely.

CHAPTER 8

Mad Max stepped out of the shower in the bathroom of his suite with a smile on his face. He slipped into his robe and made his way over to the sink. Mad Max was feeling good; so far, he had taken down over eighteen agents, and if everything went well tonight, his body count would go from eighteen to nineteen. The sound of soft piano music hummed from the small speaker that rested over on the dresser. Mad Max stepped out the bathroom and walked over towards the king sized bed where his outfit was laid out across the bed along with a suitcase. Mad Max slipped into a pair of dress pant, then placed his Kevlar vest over his under shirt and fastened the straps on the sides. Once Mad Max was fully dressed in his navy blue suit, he quickly popped open his suitcase. Inside rested a Ax50 .50 caliber sniper rifle. Mad Max quickly assembled the rifle then made his way over towards the window and opened it. Across the street in a hotel that sat adjacent from the hotel he was in sat Special Agent Mike Dansby. In the room along with Mike were two women, one blonde hair women and the other brunette. The two women seemed to enjoy their jobs as prostitutes a little too much.

***

Mike laid flat on his back in the bed while the blonde rode his face like she had a point to prove. Meanwhile, her brunette partner pleased Mike orally. The blonde gyrated her hips and moaned loudly as

Mike's tongue found her sweet spot. With each tongue, lapping the blonde's moans became louder and more desperate with each passing second. While Mike was busy pleasing the blonde the brunette pleased, Mike by treating his rod like it was an ice cream cone on a warm sunny day. Tonight was one of the best nights of Mike's life or at least he thought so.

***

Mad Max positioned his rifle on the window seal and peeked through his scope. Through the scope, Mad Max watched agent Mike Dansby, enjoy the luxury of pleasing two women at one time. He took his time enjoying a minute or two of the show before he decided to get down to business. Mad Max eased the rifle to the left until the cross hair was positioned on agent Mike's throat. Mad Max wrapped his finger around the trigger and pulled the trigger. *Thwap!* The silenced bullet exited through the rifle and traveled through the air, shattered the window, and lodged in Agent Mike's upper neck. Before the two even had a clue as to what was going on, Mad Max fired another round that hit agent Mike in the center of his heart; he wasn't taking no chances with the agent. The blonde began grinding her vagina on her clients face when a bullet entered the side of her head. The impact from the bullet caused her to violently flip off the bed. The brunette looked on with a scared and fearful look on her face. She didn't know what was going on; all she knew was whatever it was it wasn't good. The sad part was she had no clue what was going on. The brunette jumped out of the bed butt naked and called herself running out the front door. Just as she reached for the door, a bullet entered through the back of her head and exited through her eye painting the wall red.

Mad Max closed the window, closed the drapes, and quickly broke down his sniper rifle. Mad Max packed away all of his belongings, exited his room, and headed downstairs to check out. Mad Max walked out of the hotel like nothing happened and waited until the valet worker pulled his car around. "Thank you," Mad Max tipped the valet worker, got in his car, and drove away without a care in the world.

Mad Max pulled up at the red light when he felt his cell phone vibrating in his suit jacket pocket. "Yeah," he answered.

"I think it's time for you to shut down for a second," the female voice on the other line suggested. "Every cop and agent in the world is looking for you. I say you fall off the radar for a second and let them live with the fear of not knowing when you'll strike again."

"I thought this was about the money?" Mad Max questioned. "The plan was to show them we mean business then we'd have a leg to stand on when it came time to negotiate."

"Baby trust me we got these motherfuckers by the balls," she laughed. "But at the same time we don't want to put you in any danger,"

"Samantha I'm fine," Mad Max assured his girlfriend. Mad Max and Samantha had been together since they were teenagers but never got married or spoke in public due to their criminal ways. The two figured it'd be best if they kept their personal business personal.

"Well I miss you and I'm ready for you to come home," Samantha wined.

"One more hit and I'll be on my way back deal?"

"Deal but you have to handle it quickly," Samantha said in a seductive tone. "Don't want to keep me waiting long while your friend down here is soaking wet."

"One last job and I'll be home tomorrow baby."

CHAPTER 9

"NO TURNING BACK"

Angela and little Angie returned home from a long day of fun and a movie. Angela knew after little Angie got her bath, soon after she would be knocked out. Little Angie ran through the house searching for David.

"Hey, hey no running in the house," David reminded her.

"Daddy, me and Mommy went to the movies and we ate ice cream," little Angie said excitedly.

"Did you save me some?"

"No I was hungry," Little Angie laughed and ran off to her room.

"Hey baby," Angela walked up to Dave and tried to give him a kiss but he jerked his head back.

"Angela, we need to talk," Dave with a serious look on his face.

"Okay baby give me a second and let me put the baby in the bed first," Angela said as she disappeared upstairs and got little Angie ready for bed. The whole time her mind was racing. Angela had no clue what Dave wanted to talk about whatever it was she just hoped it wasn't nothing bad.

"Mommy can you read me a bedtime story? Pleeeease?" little Angie begged.

"Not tonight baby," Angela replied as she got little Angie out of the tub and wrapped her up in a towel. "Me and daddy have to talk about something so I promise I'll read you two bedtime stories tomorrow," she promised. Angela knew little Angie would be upset about not getting a bedtime story tonight but right now, that was the least of her worries. Angela had a bad feeling that whatever Dave wanted to talk about wasn't going to be pretty. Dave had a stone serious look on her face a look that Angela had never seen. After tucking little Angie in, Angela headed down the hall towards the master bedroom. She stepped inside the room and placed a phony smile on her face. "Hey baby you wanted to talk to me about something?"

"Is there something you want to tell me, Angela?" Dave asked looking Angela dead in the eyes.

"What are you talking about baby?" Angela asked. She was trying to by some time hoping that maybe Dave spill the beans on his own so she wouldn't volunteer any information.

"This the last time I'm going to ask you Angela, do you have something to tell me?" Dave snapped. "And don't you lie to me god dammit!"

"Dave you watch your language in this house and for the last time I have no idea what you're talking about!" Angela said matching Dave's tone.

"Oh you don't know what I'm talking about?" Dave said in a sarcastic tone as he reached under the bed and pulled Angela's chest from under her bed. Dave popped open the treasure chest and over fifteen guns along with several large stacks of cash stared back at him. "Is this yours?"

"Yes it belongs to me," Angela admitted with a look of shame. She hated that Dave had to find out like this but she figured it was either now or never.

"What the hell is it doing in our house?"

"It's for our protection," Angela tried to explain.

"Protection from who?" Dave asked. "The Chinese Army?"

"Very funny," Angela rolled her eyes. "Haven't you been watching the news? There's an assassin on the loose killing innocent people."

"Angela you're not making any sense," Dave yelled. "What does an assassin being on the loose have to do with us?"

"Dave it's a long story," Angela huffed. She hated talking about her past and more importantly she wasn't allowed to talk about it, the majority of Angela's job was confidential.

"It's that girl Ashley isn't it?" Dave spat. "Ever since she showed up at our house you've been acting weird. Now tell me what's going on right now or else," Dave said with a serious no nonsense look on his face.

"Or else what?" Angela challenged. She didn't do well with threats.

"Either you tell me what the hell is going on or you can get the hell out of my house!" Dave growled. He felt betrayed. Never would he have thought that Angela would be the one to keep him in the dark on a situation as serious as one like this.

"Your house?" Angela echoed. "Last time I checked this was *our* house."

"Liars aren't welcome in this house," Dave said and walked back over to the chest. "You got all these guns in this house knowing we have a child in here," Dave looked at Angela and the sight of her alone disgusted him.

"I'll get that out of here," Angela grabbed the chest and carried it downstairs. She couldn't believe how Dave was acting and was glad he showed his true colors tonight. It wasn't what Dave said that pissed Angela off, but how he said it. Dave's tone was disrespectful and borderline offensive. Angela stepped out the front door just as someone entered through the back door simultaneously.

***

Mad Max entered Dave and Angela's house through the back door. He was dressed in an all-black expensive suit, in his hands rested a submachine gun with an extended clip hanging out the base of the gun. Mad Max held a firm two-handed grip on his weapon, as he made sure the first level of the house was clear. Mad Max eased his way up the stairs one-step at a time. The closer Mad Max got to the second level of the house; he heard the sound of water running coming from the bathroom.

Dave entered the bathroom in his and Angela's bedroom and ran a shower. He stepped out of the bathroom with a frown on his face. Dave still couldn't believe that the love of his life was keeping secrets from him. They were supposed to be a team, life partners, and most importantly, they were supposed to be one. Dave removed his clothes and hopped in the shower.

Mad Max followed the sound of the shower with fire dancing in his eyes. After this last hit, Mad Max decided he would be taking a little break for a while and focus a little bit more on his personal life. Mad

Max reached the bathroom, took a deep breath, then turned, and kicked the door in. Mad Max entered the bathroom and didn't bother to pull the shower curtain back. Instead, he squeezed down on the trigger sending a series of bullets through the shower curtain. Seconds later, Mad Max snatched the curtain back and saw a man laid out in the tub, his body full of fresh bullet holes. Mad Max's target was a female, which meant he had hit the wrong target.

CHAPTER 10

"HIDE AND SEEK"

Angela walked to her car and tossed her treasure chest in the backseat of her Ford Explorer. A part of her still couldn't believe that Dave was really putting her out of their home. Angela didn't want to leave but decided to be the bigger person and leave. Besides she'd rather leave and be safe than to stay and have problems. Angela looked up and spotted a silver luxury car parked over in the cut. Angela could tell that someone was trying to be incognito. She nor Dave ever had company so the car parked over in the cut was a red flag. Angela popped open the treasure chest, grabbed a .380, and made her way back inside the house. Angela walked through the front door and immediately something didn't feel right. Angela slowly made her way upstairs. With each step Angela took, she could feel her heart trying to beat out of her chest; her palms were sweaty not to mention her adrenalin was through the roof. Angela entered her bedroom and the first red flag she noticed was that someone had kicked the bathroom door off the hinges. At first Angela thought, maybe Dave may have broken the door out of anger and frustration but after giving it some thought, Angela couldn't see Dave doing something like that. Angela stepped in the bathroom and saw Dave sprawled out butt naked in the tub, his body riddled with bullet holes. Angela covered her mouth as her eyes immediately began to water. This is why people like her never get attached or close to other people. Angela stood there trying for a second when she suddenly remembered that her daughter was also in the house. *"Oh my god little Angie!"* Angela rushed out of her bedroom when a foot came out of nowhere and kicked her gun out of her hand. The gun bounced off the wall and landed on the floor next to the stairs. Mad Max then quickly turned the business end of his gun on Angela. Just as Mad Max squeezed the trigger, Angela went low and scooped his legs from up under him, dumping Mad Max on his head as the machine gun discharged several times by accident before Mad Max lost possession of the firearm. Mad Max lifted his leg, kicked Angela off him, and then quickly climbed back on his feet. Mad Max tried to grab Angela but she swiftly swiped his hands away and landed a three-punch combo to the assassin's face. Mad Max dodged the last punch, grabbed the back of Angela's head, and delivered two strong knees to Angela's midsection. Mad Max grabbed a handful of Angela's hair and went to throw an elbow to the side of Angela's face but caught his arm in mid-stride. As the two stood in a clench, Mad Max rushed Angela backwards slamming her back hard up against the wall. Angela tried to throw a straight right hand but Mad Max weaved the punch, slipped behind Angela, and put her in a deadly chokehold from behind. Angela's head got big as she felt her oxygen being cut off. Mad Max then wrapped his legs around Angela's waist and pulled back taking both of them down to the floor. Angela felt herself losing consciousness when she looked up and saw little Angie standing in the doorway of her room watching the entire scene play out. Angela reached down in Mad Max's boot, pulled out his knife, and jammed it down into the assassin's thigh forcing him to release his grip from around her neck.

"Angie, get back in your room and close the door now!" Angela yelled as she struggled back to her feet. Angela spun around and immediately her head snapped back from the jab that Mad Max fired. Mad Max fired a series of punches followed by two strong kicks. Angela blocked the blows with her elbows and forearms then fired off two punches of her own that landed flush on Mad Max's chin. That last blow stunned Mad Max but he somehow managed to keep his footing. Angela landed a sidekick to the assassin's face that sent him flying down the stairs. Angela quickly picked her .380 up from off the floor and to little Angie's room. Angela entered her daughter's room and found little Angie sitting in the corner with her head tucked in her knees crying her eyes out. "Come on baby, we have to go!" Angela huffed as she picked little Angie up and exited the bedroom. Angela eased down the hallway as several bullets ripped through the wall. Angela quickly dove inside the master bedroom as more bullets decorated the wall. The loud gunshots scared little Angie so bad that she peed on herself and started crying at the top of her lungs.

"Shhh! It's going to be okay baby!" Angela said in a harsh whisper as she looked around for anything she could use as a weapon.

"Mommy, I'm scared. Where's daddy?" little Angie cried. Angela ignored her. Angie's mind was spinning right now; she needed to find a way to keep her daughter alive. Angela heard the assassin's footsteps getting closer and closer and all she could think about was that big machine gun he had in his possession. Having no other options, Angela grabbed little Angie and kissed her on her forehead, then without warning, she roughly grabbed little Angie and tossed her head first out of the second floor window just as Mad Max rounded the corner with his finger pressed down on the trigger of his automatic weapon. Angela sprinted across the room as a trail of bullets followed her every move. Angela dove over the bed and used one of the dressers that sat in the room as a shield. Mad Max ran and jumped over the bed and aimed his gun at Angela's head. Finally he had gotten a clean shot and wasn't about to pass up on it. Mad Max smirked as he squeezed down on the trigger.

CLICK! CLICK! CLICK!

Mad Max picked the worst time ever to run out of bullets. He quickly reached and grabbed a fresh clip from off of his utility belt and reloaded his weapon in three seconds flat, but before he got a chance to use his weapon, an elbow smashed into his face that caused him to stumble a bit and drop his weapon. Mad Max bent down to pick up his weapon when Angela kicked him in the face like she was kicking a field goal. She quickly followed with a series of punches from all different angles. Mad Max stepped back and block every blow with his elbows. Mad Max threw a faint jab at Angela's stomach then fired off a powerful right hook that landed on Angela's chin and put her down in the process. Mad Max had knocked out plenty of men with that same exact punch so when he saw Angela climbing back to her feet he had a look of disbelief on his face. Mad Max roughly grabbed Angela and rammed her head into the wall, then landed two vicious knees to Angela's stomach and chest area. Angela took the knees well and managed to land a quick uppercut to Mad Max's chin. Angela faked like she was about to throw a jab then instead threw a lightning quick head kick that bounced off the top of Mad Max's head the next kick landed in the pit of Mad Max's stomach sending him shuffling back a few steps. Angela saw her opportunity and decided to take it. She ran full speed and collided with Mad Max. Mad Max stumbled back a couple of steps as the two went crashing out the second floor window.

Angela and Mad Max both hit the ground hard and in awkward positions. Angela manage to crawl to her feet first. She was about to take off in a sprint in an attempt to try and get away from the crazy assassin when she heard little Angie crying. Angela's head snapped over to the right and spotted little Angie laid out in the bushes holding her ankle.

Angela rushed and Angie up and began to job to safety.

"Mommy, my ankle is broken!" little Angie squealed in tremendous pain.

"It's okay baby, Mommy's going to get you some help now," Angela said as she sucked up as much oxygen as she could. Angela's body was battered and bruised but she knew if she stopped moving her and, little Angie were as good as dead.

"Mommy, my leg is hurting really…"

Angela heard little Angie's voice fade in her ear as she felt a warm liquid splatter on her neck. "No…no," Angela cried as she gently laid little Angie's body down. The first thing Angela stopped was a bullet hole in little Angie's neck. Angela applied pressure on the wound but it was no use; it seemed like the more she tried to stop the bleeding the more bleed poured out of the wound. Angela looked up and spotted Mad Max running off into the woods. "Baby can you hear me? Please talk to me!" Angela yelled as she stood up and ran inside the house. She grabbed the cordless phone off its base and quickly dialed 911. Angela quickly ran back outside and cradled little Angie's head in her arms as the silent tears ran down her face. Angela looked down and couldn't believe her eyes. "I promise I'm going to kill everyone who had something to do with this!" she whispered as the sound of sirens blaring in the distance grew louder and louder with each passing second. Angela looked down at little Angie and gently kissed her forehead. "Mommy loves you, don't you ever forget that."

The paramedics rushed and began working on little Angie but it was no use she was already done. Angela stared out into space as she heard the paramedics using every trick in the book to try and revive little Angie's life. Angela stared blankly without blinking until she heard a familiar voice.

"Angela, are you okay?" Ashley asked with tears in her eyes as she sat down next to Angela and gently rubbed her back. "We're going to find this monster."

"I'm going to kill him and anyone that had anything to do with this," Angela said. She still hadn't blinked and was still staring out into space.

"Want to tell me what happened?" Ashley whispered.

"He killed my baby and my husband," Angela replied in a voice just above a whisper as the tears began to flow again. The media and several news crews pulled up to the scene turning the matter from bad to worst in a matter of seconds.

Ashley got up walked inside the house. Since Angela wasn't in a talking mood, she figured she'd go inside and see how much damage had been done with her own eyes. As soon as Ashley stepped foot inside the house, it felt empty like all of the life had been sucked out of the house. It wasn't until she made it upstairs that she could tell a big time battle had taken place. Furniture was broken and bullets holes decorated most of the walls. Another big hole was in the wall from where Angela and Mad Max must have crashed into it. Ashley strolled through the house and from all the damage she could pretty much tell what had taken place inside the house without her even being there. Ashley entered the master bedroom and the first thing she noticed was that the bathroom door had been kicked off the hinges. Ashley stepped inside the bathroom and quickly covered her mouth when she saw Dave laying lifeless in the tub. It bothered Ashley to see Dave like that especially since she knew how happy he made Angela. Angela's entire family been destroyed in one day and it was no bringing them back. Ashley walked over towards the window where Angela and Mad Max fell from and examined everything.

After inspecting the entire house, Ashley stepped back outside and rejoined Angela who sat with her head down staring at the floor while Troy rubbed her back trying to soothe her.

Troy looked up just in time to see Ashley walking up. "What's it looking like inside?"

"Like a tornado has been through there," Ashley said as they all noticed Captain Spiller walk up with a frown on his face.

"I heard about what happened and I got here as soon as I could," Captain Spiller explained. "I'm sorry for your loss, Angela. I'm sure you had a wonderful family," he paused. "You're lucky to still be alive, every other agent that has crossed paths with Mad Max they're all dead."

"Is that supposed to make me feel better?" Angela said speaking for the first time. Her eyes were blood shot red from all the crying she had been doing since her daughter and boyfriend were gunned down like an animal.

"No but I'm hoping this puts a fire under your ass," Captain Spiller said holding back no punches.

"I'm going to get straight to the point, Angela," he said looking Angela in the eyes. "Get back out there in the field and take this animal down."

Angela stood up and got face to face with Captain Spiller. "I'm going to kill him and anyone who stands in my way of accomplishing this!" she said through clenched teeth.

CHAPTER 11

"NOTHING TO TALK ABOUT"

Angela sat in an empty room with a blank expression on her face. She still couldn't believe all of the events that had taken place over the last twenty-four hours. It was as if she was living out a bad dream and she was now finally ready to wake up. Angela knew she was going to avenge the deaths of her daughter and boyfriend if it was the last thing she did. She just hoped and prayed that not too many innocent people had to lose their lives in the process. As Angela sat in the empty room, her mind began thinking back on all of the fun memories that she shared with her new family and now in one day her entire world was taking away from her with no explanation. All Angela knew about this crazy assassin was that his name was Mad Max and now his face was stuck in her memory bank and that's all she needed. Just as Angela was starting to get restless, she heard the door open and in walked Captain Spiller along with another white man.

"Hey Angela, how you feeling?" Captain Spiller asked in an even tone.

"I'm still alive," she answered in a dry tone. Right now, all Angela cared about was killing Mad Max.

"This here is Lieutenant Barkley and he's going to be helping us out with this investigation," Captain Spiller explained.

"Nice to meet you, Angela. First off, I want to say I'm sorry for your lost and I promise I'll do everything in my power to find the man who did this to your family," Lieutenant Barkley began. "Now tell me what happen from the beginning."

"I already told y'all a hundred times what happened," Angela snapped with an attitude.

"Angela if you want us to help you then I'm going to need you to cooperate," Lieutenant Barkley said matching Angela's tone.

"I don't need anyone's help," Angela replied. "Whoever this assassin is, I'm going to kill him."

"Angela you are no longer an agent," Lieutenant Barkley reminded her. "And not to mention you not being behind bars is a privilege. You're only a free woman because of this man standing next to me," he nodded towards Captain Spiller. "So if I was you I would tread lightly."

"Well you're not me," Angela countered. "I've already lost everything so your threats mean nothing to me!"

"Two things can happen here," Lieutenant Barkley said strongly. "One, you can cooperate and help us this assassin, or two, you can keep your attitude and go back into a cold jail cell the choice is yours."

"Lieutenant, can I have a word with her alone for a second please," Captain Spiller requested.

"You got two minutes," Lieutenant Barkley said on his way out.

Once it was just the two of them alone, Captain Spiller spoke. "Angela I'm going to need you to cooperate so things can go back to normal."

"Things will never be able to go back to normal," Angela countered. She didn't have time for all the mind games that they were trying to play with her.

"Angela you were only released from prison because you agreed to help the agency when we need you," Captain Spiller paused for a second. "Now I had to pull a lot of strings to get you to be able to leave and start your life over with your new family but a lot of people were against that decision and felt that if you weren't working for the agency any more then you should be back behind bars."

Angela knew the cards were stacked against her, but she refused to continue to be a slave for her freedom so whatever was going to happen was just going to happen.

"I need you to just answer any questions they may need. You to answer so things can be smooth," Captain Spiller suggested. "You know these people don't play fair."

"I told you I'm done, captain," Angela told him. "I no longer have the love to do this. Besides I'm getting old," she paused for a second. "I can't do this forever sooner or later one of those bullets are going to catch up to me."

"You're not listening to me, Angela. If you don't cooperate there's nothing I can do for you they will take you back to jail," Captain Spiller told her. "Just answer the questions and help out when we need you at least then you won't be in jail."

Angela looked Captain Spiller in the eyes. "Captain, I appreciate everything you've done for me but I'm walking out of this door and I'm going to hunt Mad Max down and kill him after that's over with I'll sit in jail for the rest of my life peacefully."

"I don't want to see you in jail, Angela. I hear what you're saying but I just don't want to see you behind bars," Captain Spiller said in a sincere tone. "Please if you don't do it for yourself then do it for me," he pleaded.

"I'm sorry captain but I can't," Angela stood firm. "I'm going to kill Mad Max."

Captain Spiller's eyes got watery as he stared at Angela for about twenty seconds. "Angela if you do something stupid they won't hesitate to kill you."

"I'm aware," Angela replied.

Captain Spiller walked up and gave Angela a big hug. "I love you,"

"I love you too captain," Angela said as she watched Captain Spiller make his exit leaving her in the room all alone. Ten minutes later, Lieutenant Barkley entered the room followed by officers all wearing riot gear.

"So Angela, what's it going to be?" Lieutenant Barkley asked with a cocky smirk on his face.

"Fuck you!" Angela spat as she stood and took a fighting stance.

"Go get her boys!" Lieutenant Barkley ordered. The first officer pulled out his baton and ran towards Angela. He swung the baton at her head with all his might. Angela quickly ducked the baton and swept the officers legs from up under him. Angela went to go stomp the man's head into the floor when she looked up and saw four more officers charging at her. The first officer hit Angela hard, lifting her off her feet then violently slamming her down to the floor. When the two hit the floor, Angela somehow managed to roll on top of the officer. She popped his helmet off and landed two strong blows to officer's face before two more officers were taking swings at her. Angela weaved and dodged the blows landing a few of her own. One of the officers managed to grab Angela and slam her against the wall. Angela quickly kneed the officer in between his legs, grabbed the back of his head, and rammed her knee into the officer's face. The next officer ran up and was greeted with a three-punch combination to the face followed by a roundhouse kick to the head. The last officer snuck up on Angela from behind. Angela spun around just as a fist landed flush on her chin. The impact from the punch put Angela on her back but it didn't put her to sleep. The officer jumped on top of Angela and began throwing wild punches. A few of punches landed but the majority of them didn't. The officer threw another punch when Angela caught his arm in mid swing and slipped it into an arm bar. Lieutenant Barkley looked on in horror as Angela snapped the officer's arm as if it was a twig.

Angela slowly stood to her feet and made her way towards Lieutenant Barkly with her fist balled up.

"Angela calm down," Lieutenant Barkley threw his hands up in surrender as he backed up into the wall. "Let me help you Angela," he pleaded. The look on his face was the look of a person on the verge of crying. "Angela, wait a second!"

Just as Angela got ready to strike the lieutenant, her body stiffened up like a board then collapsed hard to the floor. Behind Angela, one of the officer's stood with a taser in his hand. Lieutenant Barkley quickly jumped on Angela and handcuffed her hands behind her back.

"You silly ass cunt!" Lieutenant Barkley snapped. "All you had to do was cooperate!"

Seconds later, several more officers ran inside the room and carried Angela out.

CHAPTER 12

"BAD MOVIE"

The officer's roughly tossed Angela in the empty cell. Her hands were still cuffed behind her back, so when Angela fell, she couldn't even use her hands to protect herself or slow down her fall. Angela hit the floor and quickly rolled on her back and stared up at the ceiling. When she woke up in the morning, Angela never would have thought this was how her day was going to play out. It seemed like no matter how hard she tried to leave the game it always somehow figured out a way to get her jammed up in some shit. Angela continued to stare up at the ceiling as thoughts of little Angie flooded her mind. Angela cracked a smile not even realizing that she was smiling. She missed her boyfriend, Dave, but most importantly she missed little Angie. Angela wished the two of them could have somehow switched places that way she would be dead instead of a minor. The more and more Angela thought about the entire situation the more she realized that she couldn't bring people back from the dead. As Angela laid on her back, she heard a familiar voice say. "Are you okay?"

Angela looked up and saw Ashley standing on the other side of the bars.

"Yes I'm fine, thank you for asking," Angela replied keeping it short and sweet.

"So what's the plan?" Ashley asked. She knew Angela was the type of person that always had a plan so she knew there was no way Angela was going to just sit around and do nothing about the situation.

"I'm going to get out of here and kill Mad Max and anyone standing in my way of doing so," Angela stated plainly. All she could think about was getting revenge for her family.

"Well I'm in so tell me what you need me to do," Ashley said in a strong whisper.

"Ashley," Angela began. "You have your entire life ahead of you. This is something I have to do alone."

"Bullshit!" Ashley snapped. "We are family and we'll always be family, so the way I see it is Mad Max killed *our* family," Ashley said in a firm tone.

"Once I get out of here I'll be a fugitive," Angela explained. "I have chosen my path and I refuse to choose yours for you."

"You're not choosing nothing for me!" Ashley snapped. "You are my family pointblank – period! And I refuse to let you go and do this on your own," Ashley said as she discreetly tossed a handcuff key down by Angela's hip. "I'll be out front in a black

Camaro in five minutes," Ashley turned and walked off leaving Angela with a lot to think about.

Angela squirmed on her back until she was able to reach the key. She fumbled around with the key for a few seconds before she finally freed herself from the handcuffs. Angela walked up to the bars on her cell and called for an officer to come. "C.O.!" she yelled repeatedly until a heavyset officer turned the corner with a frustrated look on her face. Angela stood with her hands behind her back pretending to still be cuffed.

"What the hell you over here yelling about?" the officer barked.

"I need some water," Angela said. "Y'all got me over here dying of thirst." Once the officer got within arm's reach, Angela reached out and grabbed the officer by the collar of his shirt pulling him towards her forcing his head to bang violently against the steel bars on the cell. The officer hit the floor hard as blood spilled from a deep gash on his forehead.

Angela reached down and removed the officer's keys from off the man's belt. Angela let herself out the cell, quickly removed the 9mm from the officer's holster, and headed for the exit. Angela walked with her head down hoping not to get recognized but the first officer she passed stopped her.

"Hey!" the officer grabbed Angela's shoulder. Angela spun and hit the officer in the face with the butt of the 9mm. The officer went down quickly and easily as blood flowed from his nose like a faucet. Angela turned towards the exit and saw two more officers reaching for their weapons. Angela wasted no time putting the two officers down with headshots. Angela quickly hopped over the two dead bodies and broke out into a full sprint towards the exit. Angela made it a few feet away from the exit when she was tackled hard from behind. The officer placed his forearm up under Angela's chin and applied pressure. Angela shoved the business end of the 9mm into the gut of the officer and didn't hesitate to pull the trigger. Angela tossed the officer's dead body off of her and ran out the front door like a mad woman. Once outside, she spotted the black Camaro waiting for her out front. As soon as Angela's butt hit the passenger seat Ashley gunned the engine, recklessly pulling out into traffic.

"Hold on!" Ashley said as she jerked the wheel hard to the left making a sharp turn. The Camaro's engine roared as it picked up speed. Ashley drove the Camaro as if it was a racecar.

"It's not too late for you to bail out," Angela said. "You can let me out right there on the corner."

"We in this together," Ashley said keeping her eyes on the road. She knew all Angela was trying to do was look out for her but there was no way she would leave Angela high and dry especially in a time of need like this. "I have a nice low key spot for us to lay low at."

Angela sat in the passenger seat staring out into space. Ever since her family had been murdered, she found herself zoning out every now and then. Images of Mad Max's face continued to haunt her.

"You alright over there?" Ashley asked noticing that Angela didn't seem like herself.

Angela snapped out of her trance and nodded. "Yeah I'm good."

Ashley pulled the Camaro over on a quiet block and killed the engine. "Come on we have to switch cars," Ashley walked over to an old Honda and used her elbow to break the driver's side window. Once inside the car, Ashley quickly hotwired it and pulled off smoothly.

CHAPTER 13

"WHAT HAPPENED?"

Lieutenant Barkley walked through the police station with a disgusted look on his face. Laid out before him were the dead bodies of several officers that died by the hands of Angela. Lieutenant Barkley turned and looked at Captain Spiller. "I thought you told me you could trust her?"

"I've never once had a problem out of Angela," Captain Spiller replied honestly. "She's one of my best agents."

"She's a fucking convict!" Lieutenant Barkley barked. "You put your name and the entire department on the line for a common criminal!"

"Are you forgetting that a crazy assassin just murdered her family?" Captain Spiller reminded him. "Angela is a killer and she's not going to stop until that assassin that murdered her family is dead!"

"Angela is a liability that needs to be dealt with," Lieutenant Barkley said not hiding the fact that he didn't care for or like Angela. "She assaulted several officers then killed several more right up under our noses!"

"Lieutenant, I just think…"

"Fuck what you think!" Lieutenant Barkley yelled cutting Captain Spiller off in mid-sentence. "You're suspended until further notice, and just so you know my men will be given the order to terminate on sight, now get the fuck out outta here!" he said in a dismissive tone. Lieutenant Barkley walked back to his office and shut the door behind him. "Fuck!" Lieutenant Barkley cursed as he pulled out his cell phone and dialed a number. On the fourth ring, Samantha answered in a soft tone.

"Hello,"

"What the fuck is going on!" Lieutenant Barkley yelled into the phone. "We had a fucking deal!"

"Lieutenant Barkley, please calm down," Samantha said in an even tone. "Look, me and my husband got rid of enough agents as it is already. His trail started getting hot so I told him to let it cool off."

"Put your husband on the phone!" Lieutenant Barkley barked. Seconds later, Mad Max's voice came on the other line.

"Yeah what's up?"

"Out of all people you let the Teflon Queen escape? How the hell did you let that happen?"

"I could have taken her out but the cops showed up sooner than I expected," Mad Max told him. "She's good but she ain't that good."

"Well we had her in custody and now she's escaped," Lieutenant Barkley explained. "She killed several of my men on her way out and now she coming for you."

Mad Max laughed loudly. "Let her come," he said as if it wasn't a big deal that one of the best agents in the world had a bullet with his name on it.

"Listen, Angela is no joke!" Lieutenant Barkley stated plainly. "Watch your back and I'll be in touch," Lieutenant Barkley ended the call hanging up in Mad Max's ear.

***

Ashley pulled up in front of a nice single family home and quickly pulled in the garage. Once the garage door was fully closed, both women stepped out of the stolen vehicle.

"Whose house is this?" Angela asked curiously, as she looked around.

"This is Troy's secret getaway house," Ashley said as she let herself inside the house. "He keeps this house as an emergency house and I think this would classify as an emergency."

Angela walked through the house looking around. It was a nice place, a little small and cozy, but still nice. "You sure Troy is going to be okay with us staying here for a few days?"

Ashely waved her off. "Troy don't care," she said nonchalantly. "I keep telling you we all family," she said as she raided the fridge. "You hungry?"

"Starving," Angela replied as she sat down on the sofa, leaned her head back, and closed her eyes. She had been up for the last four days without sleep and her body was ready to shut down.

"Okay you want a sandwich, chicken, or fish?" Ashley asked. When she looked over in Angela's direction, she heard light snoring from the couch. Ashley walked over towards the linen closet, grabbed a sheet, and covered Angela with it. Ashley knew that Angela had been through a lot in these past couple of days. Ashley wished it were something she could have done to prevent these things from happening but now it was a little too late to cry over spilled milk. While Ashley stood in the kitchen frying fish, she heard the front door open and saw Troy walk through the front door.

"I got your text, what's the emergency?" Troy asked. Ashley nodded over towards the couch. Troy's eyes traveled to the couch and all he could do was shake his head. "I should have known."

"She didn't have anywhere else to go," Ashley handed Troy a plate of chicken hoping that would put him in a better mood.

"Every cop in the world is looking for Angela and you bring her here?" Troy said. He didn't see anything good coming from this situation. "They kick this door down right now and you do know that all three of us will be thrown in jail for the rest of our lives right?"

"It's cool, I'll leave," Angela got up from the couch and headed for the door.

"Angela wait!" Troy stopped her. "I can't let you go out there on your own like that," he escorted her back towards the kitchen area. "We all in this together."

"I need all the information you can find on Mad Max," Angela said as she bit down into a piece of chicken. "And I need a gun and a lot of ammo."

"Done," Troy walked over to the kitchen table, pulled out his laptop, and began clicking away. "Okay, so Mad Max was last seen in Italy."

Angela nodded her head as she continued to destroy her chicken. "What else?"

"He likes expensive wines," Troy looked up for a response.

"Any family?"

Troy punched some keys on the computer, moved the mouse around a few times, and then looked up at Angela. "Says he has a sister."

"Where?"

"His sister lives in Miami," Troy said with a smile. He pulled out a piece of paper, scribbled down the address, and handed it to Angela. "That should be a good place to start."

CHAPTER 14

"MEXICO"

Mad Max sat at the bar at a nice hotel. He had been staying in this same hotel out in Mexico for the past four days. His target was a woman named Crystal Montgomery. Crystal was an eyewitness, scheduled to testify against a big fish, and threatened to take down a large powerful organization. That's when Mad Max was hired to get rid of her. Mad Max looked around the bar and noticed two men over in the cut watching Crystal's every move but pretended to be conversating with each other when they were really there to make sure nothing happened to the witness. Mad Max played it cool and continued to sip his drink as he watched Crystal's every move. If the witness only had two guys protecting her then this was going to be easier than he had anticipated. Mad Max double-checked his surroundings to make sure there were only two protecting the witness. *"Yup just those two,"* he said to himself as he finished up his drink, paid his tab, and exited the bar. Mad Max slipped on the elevator and got off on the seventh floor. Mad Max walked down the carpeted hallway then dipped off in the staircase; he quickly knocked down the camera then pulled his .380 from the small of his back and attached a silencer onto the barrel. Now all he had to do was wait.

***

Crystal Montgomery paid her tab at the bar then headed for the elevators. All the wine she drank was starting to run through her. Crystal entered the elevator along with her two personal bodyguards. "Y'all need to loosen up," Crystal slurred. "No one is going to come all the way to Mexico to kill me,"

"Better safe than sorry," one of the bodyguards replied shortly.

"I guess," Crystal waved him off as the trio exited the elevator and headed down the hall when the staircase door busted open and a man in a dark suit stepped out with a black gun in his hand. Mad Max dropped both the bodyguards with headshots before they even got a chance to get to their weapons. Crystal went to scream but Mad Max sent a bullet in her throat, her scream never made it out. Crystal melted down to her knees in slow motion, her eyes bulging wide. Mad Max finished the witness off with a head shot. Before Mad Max could disappear into the staircase, a nosey neighbor stuck his head out the door. Mad Max shot the elderly man in the face, and then fled in the staircase not even waiting for the man's body to hit the floor. Mad Max nonchalantly trotted down the stairs as he unscrewed the silencer, removed it from the barrel, and slipped it down in his pocket. He then shoved his .380 in the holster in the small of his back. Mad Max reached the lobby and blended in with the rest of the guests. Mad Max stepped out the hotel and got in a cab. "Take me to the airport please," he said in a cool tone as he discreetly placed his gun and silencer on the floor of the cab. Mad Max pulled out his phone and sent his wife a quick one-word text message. *"Done,"* Mad Max sat in the back of the cab and replayed the conversation he had with Lieutenant Barkley over again in his mind. *"She killed several men on her way out and now she's coming for you."* Lieutenant Barkley's voice played over and over. Mad Max did his homework on the Teflon Queen and knew she wouldn't stop until his brains were on the curb somewhere. Mad Max planned to be prepared for the Teflon Queen whenever she decided to show up but in the meantime, it was business as usual. When it was time to cross that bridge, Mad Max planned on handling the situation.

CHAPTER 15

"MIAMI"

Angela sat in the driver seat of her rental car with a serious look on her face. After a three-hour conversation, Angela finally convinced Ashley and Troy to stay behind and not involve themselves this go round. Angela didn't want any blood on their hands especially since she planned on getting down and dirty until she found Mad Max. The entire situation felt unreal to Angela. She was used to waking up to kissing Dave and the soft voice of little Angie. Now it seemed like every time she woke up it was in a cold sweat. Angela pulled the rental car in the empty CVS parking lot and waited as if Ashley had instructed her to do. Four minutes later, another car pulled up and a scrawny man stepped out and entered the passenger side of Angela's car carrying a duffle bag in his hand.

"Sorry I'm late," the scrawny man said in a fast tone. "Had to go grab something to eat first," he said then sat the duffle bag on Angela's lap. "Everything you need is in that bag."

Angela unzipped the duffle bag and peeked inside. She then handed the scrawny man a thick wad of cash in exchange for the bag.

The scrawny man thumbed through the cash then looked up and smiled. "Tell Ashley I appreciate the business. If she ever needs me, don't be afraid to call," the scrawny man said then exited the vehicle leaving Angela alone in her thoughts. Angela quickly backed out of the parking lot and continued on to her destination. Angela rode on the highway doing the speed limit listening to the radio when she noticed flashing blue lights in her rear view mirror. "Shit!" Angela cursed as she pulled over to the side of the road. The first thing that popped into Angela's mind was the scrawny guy must have ratted her out. There was a five million dollar reward out for anyone who had any information about Angela's whereabouts. Angela grabbed her fake license and rolled her window down as the officer made his way her driver side window.

"License and registration please ma'am," the officer said in a strong tone.

"What seems to be the problem officer?"

"License and registration please!" the officer repeated in an even louder tone. Not wanting to cause any drama, Angela handed the officer the paper work he requested. "Here you go."

The officer took the documents and headed back to his squad car. Once the officer was back in his car Angela reached over in the duffle bag that sat in the passenger's seat and removed a 9mm. She made sure the magazine was full before cocking a round into the chamber. Angela looked through her rear view mirror and noticed two more cop cars pull up. Immediately, Angela knew that something wasn't right and she wasn't about to sit around and wait for the cops to make their move. Without warning, Angela stepped out of her car and sent several bullets through the window of the first squad car. She didn't know if she had killed the first officer on the scene but from the way his chest jerked back and forth, she knew her bullets had found her intended target. Angela sent two more shots in the direction of the other two cars then took off running down into the woods with the duffle bag over her shoulder. The other two officers quickly took off in the woods after Angela. The two officers ran in the woods then stopped; they looked around and didn't see or hear anything. "You go that way and I'll go this way," the shorter officer out of the two said. The shorter officer eased his way through the woods with each step he took it announced his location as he stepped on a bunch of leaves and broken twigs. The officer walked through the woods and stopped when he felt an acorn hit him on the shoulder. The officer looked up and saw Angela up in the tree above him. Before the officer could react, Angela jumped down out of the tree and jammed a sharp hunting knife deep into the neck of the officer.

***

The taller officer walked through the woods and stopped when he heard a scream coming from the other end of the woods. He wasn't too sure but he of sworn that the voice of the scream sounded like it belonged to his fellow officer. The taller officer quickly ran through the woods in the direction that the scream had come from and stopped when he saw his fellow officer laying on the ground with a huge hole in his neck. The officer then suddenly collapsed when a bullet exploded in his thigh. "Urghh!" the officer growled as he rolled around on the ground holding his thigh. He heard the sound of leaves crunching getting closer and closer until he looked up and saw the Teflon Queen standing over him with the barrel of a gun aimed at his face.

"Please don't do this," the officer pleaded with a frightened look on his face. "I just had a new born..."

Blocka!

Angela fired a shot into the officer's face showing no mercy. She then grabbed her duffle bag and continued on towards her destination. Angela refused to let anything slow her down or stop her from completing her mission. Whoever tried to stand in her way would have a hell of a price to pay.

***

Angela sat in a small coffee shop with a baseball cap pulled down low, a pair of dark sunglasses covered her eyes, and a newspaper laid in front of her just in case she needed to use it. She sipped on her tea and looked up at the TV that hung over the counter. On the TV was a reporter speaking about the three officers that Angela had gunned down. The reporter informed Angela that they were looking for a woman that was armed and dangerous. Two seconds later, a picture of Angela popped up on the TV with the words *"Wanted,"* above her picture. Angela quickly paid her tab and exited the small coffee shop. With the way things were looking, she knew she wouldn't be able to stay in Miami for long.

CHAPTER 16

"LAST CHANCE"

Linda Hernandez stood in the kitchen of her home sipping on a glass of red wine. She'd had a long day in the office and couldn't wait to unwind. Linda walked through the house freely and in the nude. She entered her bedroom then stepped out onto her private balcony and took in the view and inhaled the fresh air. Linda raised her glass up to her mouth and took another sip of wine when she noticed a pair of headlights pull into her driveway. Linda squinted her eyes to try and get a better look at whom the driver was. What really puzzled Linda was the fact that she rarely had any guess; especially guess that showed up to her house unannounced. After further investigation, Linda realized that the driver of the car was none other than Frank her ex-boyfriend. "Frank the hell are you doing here?" Linda yelled from the balcony.

"Baby we need to talk!" Frank stepped out of the carrying a dozen white roses and an *"I'm sorry"* look on his face.

"We don't have nothing to talk about and I'm not your baby!" Linda shot back. It had been two weeks since Linda had come home early from work and found Frank in their bed with the neighbor's daughter. That was the last time Linda laid eyes on Frank up until now.

"Come on baby, open up!" Frank yelled up towards the balcony. "At least let me give you these roses," he took a strong whiff of the flowers. "Mmm."

"Frank you can take those flowers and shove them up your ass!" Linda shot back. The truth was she did miss Frank and wanted to give him another chance, but deep down inside she knew he wasn't ever going to change.

Knowing that if she didn't talk to Frank, he'd probably stand outside all night making noise. Linda decided to go downstairs and let him in for a second. She walked downstairs, opened the door with an attitude, and snatched the flowers out of Frank's hands. "You got five minutes so make it good," she stepped to the side so Frank could enter.

"Let me make this right baby," Frank melted down to his knees and began to kiss Linda's feet. "Baby, I'll do anything to make this back right again," he begged.

"It was already right until you decided to go out mess it up," Linda spat with her arms folded across her chest. "I'll never be able to trust you again."

"But baby…" Frank's voice stopped when he looked past Linda and saw another woman standing in the foyer dressed in all black. "What the hell is going on?" Frank stood back up to his feet. "What you into girls now?" He nodded towards the woman in all black.

Linda turned around and saw the woman standing in the foyer. Instantly, she recognized the woman from the news as being armed and dangerous. "What are you doing here?" Linda asked. "Get out of my house now before I call the cops," she threatened.

Angela pulled a 9mm from the small of her back and slowly inched her way towards the couple. "I didn't come here to hurt anyone I just came here for some information."

"Hey, fuck you!" Frank spat as he pulled Linda behind him. "What you think I'm scared because you got a little gun? It's probably not even real."

Blocka!

The gun roared as a bullet struck Frank in the leg dropping him right where he stood. "Okay, okay, okay!" Frank cried like a girl.

Angela trained her weapon on Linda. "I don't care about you; I'm here for your brother."

"My brother?" Linda echoed with a confused look on her face. "I haven't talked to my brother in years."

"I want his real name and an address," Angela spat.

"Wait I think he needs an ambulance," Linda said with a scared look on her face.

Angela aimed her weapon at Frank's foot and pulled the trigger.

Blocka!

"Awhhhh!" Frank howled from the pain that shot through his body.

"Name and address," Angela said in a calm tone as she tossed Linda a piece of paper and a pen.

"His real name is Chad Hernandez and the last place I remember him living was Paris but that was over six years ago," Linda said. "My brother was into some bad things and I didn't want nothing to do with it so I disowned him," Linda said with a shrug.

Angela aimed her weapon at Frank's other foot. "You better come better than that!" she barked. "Who does he work for? Who's he fucking? His best friend? I want to know everything about him!"

"Last time I spoke to him he was fooling with some girl named Samantha Hancock," Linda told her. "Me and that bitch never got along she was one of those girls that thought she was too smart for her own good, a real prick."

"What does Samantha do for a living?"

"She had one of those secretive jobs," Linda said trying to remember.

"Secretive jobs doing what?" Angela pressed.

"I think was working for the FBI at the time if I'm remembering correctly."

As soon as the words left Linda's mouth, Angela's wheel began to turn in her head. Now it was all starting to make perfect sense. If Mad Max's girlfriend worked for the FBI then she definitely was able to help him sneak into the headquarters in London and infiltrate the whole system. Angela pulled out her burner phone and called Troy. On the second ring, he picked up. "Hey what's up?"

"I need info on a woman named Samantha Hancock," Angela said. "Yeah she's Mad Max's wife."

"Excellent she should lead us right to him," Troy said in an excited tone.

"Hit me back when you find out more info," Angela ended the call. She spun around and stumbled as a blunt object crashed over the top of Angela's head.

Linda hit Angela over the head with a glass ashtray. She knew Angela was a wanted woman and figured there was no way that the assassin would ever let her live so she decided to take her chances.

Angela got up off the floor and chased Linda down. She jumped on Linda's back violently tackling her down to the floor. The two hit the floor hard and slid a few feet before coming to a stop. Linda somehow managed to get to her feet first. She threw a wild haymaker at Angela's head. Angela ducked the punch and landed a strong two-piece to Linda's body. She grabbed Linda's head and rammed it into the wall. Angela then landed a series of elbows to Linda's face then let out an animalistic growl as she snapped Linda's neck.

Angela stormed back into the kitchen area and pumped four slugs into Frank's chest then turned and made her exit.

***

Angela entered her motel room, kicked her boots off, and flopped down on the bed. She was exhausted and was ready to get some much-needed rest. Angela placed her 9mm within arm's reach on the bed and shut her eyes. She tried her best not think about Dave and little Angie but that task was easier said than done. Just as Angela drifted off into a good sleep, she was quickly awakened by a loud banging sound coming from the room next door. Angela quickly jumped up and grabbed her 9mm. When she realized it was a false alarm she laid back down. Angela tried to go back to sleep but the sound of a man yelling at the top of his lungs followed by the sound of a slap filled the air. Then Angela heard a woman crying and begging the man to stop hitting her. Angela tried to ignore the screams but the walls in the motel were as thin as paper making it easy for Angela to hear the woman in the next room getting beat on.

Angela signed loudly as she stood, put her boots back on, and exited her room.

***

In the next room, Bobby stood over Valerie with a mean look on his face. "Where's the rest of my money bitch?"

"Daddy, I'm sorry but it's been raining all night," Valerie pleaded. With Valerie being a prostitute the bad weather played a big part in her money coming up short. "I'll go back out and won't come back until I have all your money, Daddy."

"Oh so you stashing on me now?" Bobby ignored everything Valerie had just said. The truth of the matter was Bobby didn't really care about the money being short, he was really pissed off about losing a few hundred dollars in a dice game not too long ago, and unfortunately for Valerie he had no one else to take his anger out on but her. "You think I'm stupid or something?"

"No Daddy, I would never..." Bobby smacked the taste out of Valerie's mouth in mid-sentence.

"What did I tell you about disobeying me?" Bobby growled as he stood over Valerie in an intimidating manner. Valerie prepared herself for another blow when someone kicked the room door open with force. Valerie looked up and saw a woman in all black standing in the doorway holding some type of object that glittered in her hand.

"Bitch, who the fuck are you!" Bobby growled turning his attention to the chick dressed in all black.

"Your worst nightmare," Angela said as she stepped inside the room and closed the door behind her. Just as Bobby got ready to say another word, Angela rushed him. Before Bobby knew what was going on, Angela had already cut him four different times.

"You fucking bitch!" Bobby growled as he stumbled back into the wall. The sight of his own blood caused him to panic. "Call me an ambulance!" he demanded.

Angela ignored the sleazy pimp and slapped him down to the floor like he had done so many of his victims.

"You filthy bitch!" Bobby barked. "When I get up I'm going to gut you like a fish!" he threatened with fire dancing in his eyes. Angela raised her foot and kicked Bobby's face into the wall.

"That's enough!" Valerie cried from over in the corner. Even though Bobby used and abused her, she still loved him and didn't want to see him get hurt.

Angela turned and looked at the prostitute like she was crazy, she knew the first thing that a pimp did was mind fuck all of his women and it was obvious that Valerie fell into that category.

"Please don't hurt him anymore!" Valerie cried her eyes out. The sight of Bobby laying on the floor bleeding was crushing her on the inside. "He needs an ambulance!"

As bad as Angela wanted to finish the sleazy pimp off, she decided to just mind her business and leave the couple alone and let them handle their own affairs. Angela left the couple alone and went back to her room where she packed up all of her things and got out of dodge before one of the nosey neighbors called the cops because of the noise complaint.

Angela broke into one of the cars parked in the lot, hotwired it, and headed straight for the airport. She got on the highway and dialed Troy's number. "Hey you got any new info for me?"

"Yeah I was just about to call you," Troy said in an excited tone. "We found Mad Max, he's on vacation in Jamaica; I just got word from Captain Spiller."

"I need an address to the hotel he's staying in," Angela said quickly.

"Captain Spiller has an undercover agent with eyes on Mad Max as we speak," Troy told her. "The undercover has been given the green light to go in for the kill."

"Is the agent male or female?" Angela asked.

"Female."

"You think she has what it takes to pull it off?" Angela asked pulling into the airport parking lot.

"She's the best female agent we have besides you and Ashley."

"Why didn't Captain Spiller send Ashley?" Angela asked curiously.

"Because Mad Max would have recognized Ashley," Troy went on to explain the first run in Ashley and Mad Max's had.

"This female agent, you think she's going to be able to get the job done?" Angela asked.

"We'll know within the next few hours."

CHAPTER 17

"VACATION"

Mad Max sat on the beach reading a good book. He had been putting in so much work that he decided that a vacation was well needed. His destination was Jamaica. Mad Max loved the food, music, weather, and he most definitely enjoyed the women. Mad Max looked up from his book when he spotted a sexy blonde hair woman heading in his direction.

"Excuse me," the blonde said in a polite time. "I don't mean to bother you but I need to ask you for a favor."

"I'm listening," Mad Max sat up immediately; his eyes scanned the area looking to make sure the woman was alone. After making sure that the blonde hair woman was alone, he felt a little more comfortable. "How can I help you?"

"Do you mind rubbing some lotion on my back for me," the blonde said with a bright smile.

Mad Max smiled. "Of course I don't mind," he poured the lotion in his hand and began slowly rubbing his hands together. Instead of just rubbing lotion on the blonde's back, Mad Max took it a step further and gave her a strong-handed massage as he rubbed the lotion on her back all at the same time.

"Oh my god that feels so good," the blonde moaned in a sexually charged tone. "I see when it comes to putting lotion on a girl's back you're a professional."

"I aim to please," Mad Max shot back as he slowly glided his hands down the blonde's back stopping just above the crack of her ass. "Your thighs look a little dry too," Mad Max said in a smooth tone as he poured some more lotion in his hands and moved his hands from the blonde's back down to her healthy looking thighs. "So you live out here?"

"Hmmp!" the blonde signed. "I wish. Unfortunately I'm out here on vacation and tomorrow is my last night here."

"Well then I'm going to have to move a little quicker than I expected and ask you out to dinner right now before you make some other plans," Mad Max flashed a million dollar smile.

The blonde returned his smile. "How you going to ask me out to dinner and you don't even know my name?"

"How rude of me. The name is Michael, Michael Brow," he said the first name that came to his mind. "And you are?

"Rebecca," she extended her hand.

"Nice to meet you Rebecca," Mad Max said gently kissing the back of Rebecca's hand.

"I have my eye on you; you're a charmer," Rebecca smiled. "So what you doing out here in Jamaica? You out here with your wife?"

Mad Max laughed loudly. "Do you see a ring on my finger? Because I don't."

"Hey it's not a crime to ask a question," Rebecca said as the two shared a laugh. It was hard for agent Rebecca Strong to smile in the face of a man that was responsible for killing several of her fellow agents in cold blood. Execution style. "So what's your plans for the rest of the day?"

"I didn't have any," Mad Max replied. "Unless it's something that you would like to do?"

"Wanna go jet skiing?" Rebecca suggested trying to think of a way to get him alone and in the open where she was going to kill him and avenge the death of all of her fellow comrades.

"Can you swim?"

"Like a fish," Rebecca replied as the two ran out to the water and prepared for some fun in the sun.

***

Angela sat on the plane with the brim of her baseball cap pulled low to hide her identity. She wanted Mad Max dead but a part of her wanted the agent to fail so she could have the opportunity to kill the assassin herself. While on the plane, Angela looked up the hotel that Mad Max was currently staying at and did some research. Angela decided to close her eyes and get some rest she knew she couldn't control the situation so instead of stressing she just decided to pray for the best. The Teflon Queen was scheduled to arrive in Jamaica in four hours.

***

Rebecca held on to Mad Max's waist tightly as the Jet Ski bounced off one wave after another. "Go faster!" she yelled in Mad Max's ear. The Jet Ski roared as it picked up speed taking them further out into the ocean. Rebecca held on to Mad Max from behind and began formulating a plan on how she could take the assassin out. Right now was the perfect time; it was just the two of them out in the middle of the ocean by themselves. Rebecca looked around and saw nothing but opportunity. She silently counted to three, and then took a deep breath. Without warning, Rebecca wrapped her arms around Mad Max's neck putting him in a chokehold. She squeezed her arms as tight as she could applying as much pressure as possible. Rebecca had choked many men out using this same exact chokehold in the past.

"Arghh!" Mad Max growled as he took his hands off the handlebars and tried to remove Rebecca's arms from around his neck. In the mist of the struggle, Mad Max lost control of the Jet Ski. The Jet Ski hit a big wave and sent the two airborne violently crashing into the water. Rebecca and Mad Max went under water and continued their battle. Rebecca wrapped her legs around Mad Max's waist and continued to apply pressure to the chokehold.

Mad Max grabbed a hand full of Rebecca's hair with one hand and tried to dig her eyes out with his other hand. Rebecca did her best to ignore the pain and not release her grip from around Mad Max's neck.

Mad Max struggled and fought until finally he had passed out from the chokehold. Once Rebecca saw Mad Max's body go limp, she quickly released her chokehold and swam back up above water. Rebecca gasped for air as she held Mad Max's body with one hand and paddled with her arm. Rebecca looked at how far the shore was from where she was and almost died. It would take her forever to swim back to shore especially with her towing Mad Max's body. Seven minutes into her swim, Rebecca spotted a small lifeguard boat cruising not too far away from her. "Heeeeeey!" she yelled wailing her arms from side to side. "Over here!" Rebecca yelled, splashed water, and did anything else that she could think of until she finally got the boat's attention.

The lifeguard on the boat quickly turned the boat in the direction of a woman who looked to be stranded wailing her arms from side to side. When the boat got close, the lifeguard tossed a small rescue buoy out into the water. Rebecca quickly grabbed onto the raft as the lifeguard pulled her and Max Mad towards the boat. The lifeguard helped Rebecca onto the small boat first then he helped pull Mad Max onto the boat next. "What were y'all doing all the way out here?" the lifeguard asked in a strong Jamaican accent.

"We fell off of our jet ski," Rebecca said as she noticed Mad Max beginning to come back around. "Hey you have any handcuffs on this boat?"

"Handcuffs?" the lifeguard repeated as his face crumbled up. "Me no have none on boat."

Rebecca placed a knee into Mad Max's chest keeping him pinned down. "Do you have any rope or anything I can use to tie him up?" Rebecca asked in a desperate tone.

"Rope?" the lifeguard said with a confused look on his face. "Why tie the man up?"

Mad Max had come all the way back around but decided to play possum to see what was what and who was who. When Rebecca was, least expecting it, Mad Max forcefully pushed her knee off his chest and climbed back to his feet. Mad Max hit Rebecca with a series of blows to the face and head area as the small boat began to rock wildly from all the movement. Rebecca tried to counter with a few blows of her own but Mad Max blocked her blows with ease. Rebecca threw a jab then followed up with a sweeping hook Mad Max blocked the jab, ducked the hook, and grabbed Rebecca and tossed her over his head out into the water. Rebecca's body hit the water with a loud splash. Mad Max watched Rebecca sink down into the water when he felt a stick shattered across his back. Mad Max slowly spun around and looked at the lifeguard who held the bottom half of the broken paddle in his hand. Mad Max's hand shot out and grabbed the lifeguard by his shirt pulling the man towards him. He quickly spun the lifeguard around, grabbed his neck, and gave it a strong twist. A loud popping sound followed. Mad Max then tossed the lifeguard's lifeless body off the boat. The sound of water splashing grabbed Mad Max's attention he looked over to his right and saw Rebecca swimming further out into the ocean and away from the boat.

"I'm going to get you bitch!" Mad Max growled as the boat quickly separated the distance between them and Rebecca. Ten minutes later, the boat crashed against the shore. Mad Max jumped off the boat down onto the sand and sprinted back towards his hotel room then thought about it; if the blonde hair agent knew where to find him then there had to be others out there. *"The blonde chick is definitely not alone out here."* Mad Max said to himself as he changed directions. Instead of going back to his hotel room, Mad Max jogged over towards the gift shop and sneakily grabbed a hat, Hawaiian shirt, and a dark pair of sunglasses off the mannequin as he passed by. He tried his best to blend in with the rest of the single people and couples. Mad Max looked over his shoulder and noticed a man walking behind him talking into his wrist a straight give away.

Mad Max turned the corner, placed his back up against the wall, and patiently waited. Not having a weapon, Mad Max had no choice but to use his survival skills. When the man spun around the corner, Mad Max hit him with a quick rabbit punch. The punch dazed the man and had him out on his feet. Mad Max then quickly pulled the agent's gun from his holster and shot the man three times in the chest with his own gun and kept it moving like nothing ever happened. Mad Max quickly dashed inside a building before being spotted by any of the other several agents that were out there gunning for him.

***

The cab stopped directly in front of the hotel that Mad Max was staying in. Angela paid the driver, stepped out the back seat, and entered the hotel. She wore a baseball cap pulled down low along with a pair of dark shades. Angela was here on a mission and one mission only and that was to kill Mad Max. She boarded the elevator, pressed the floor she was looking for, and patiently waited. Angela rode up in the elevator in silence playing out the scene in her head. She stepped off the elevator, pulled the P89 from her holster, and headed straight for the room that Mad Max was staying in. Angela reached the room and placed an ear to the door. Angela shot the lock off the door, then barged inside with a two handed grip on her weapon. Angela quickly surveyed the room making sure the coast was clear before slipping her weapon back down into her holster. Angela searched Mad Max's room looking for any clue that could possibly give her a heads up on what his next move may be. Angela found a duffle bag filled with all types of weapons. A bottle of red wine rested on the nightstand along with a Rolex watch and a wallet. Angela picked up the wallet and began to search through it. Inside she found several different driver licenses. Each ID had Mad Max's face on it with a different name for each card. Angela continued to search through the wallet when she heard the sound of several footsteps coming down the hall. Angela pulled her weapon from her holster and aimed it at the door. Two men in FBI jackets came barging into the room and Angela quickly put them down with headshots. A third member came into the room, a woman and a bullet immediately exploded into her vest sending her crashing against the wall. Angela knew that the FBI were here for Mad Max and not her, but she knew by her being in Mad Max's room that would open up a lot of questions that would lead to her being arrested and Angela couldn't allow that to happen. Angela made her way to the door when another agent ran inside. Angela fired off a shot. A bullet exploded in the agents shoulder as he tackled Angela down to the floor. Angela quickly rolled on the floor, flipping the agent over in the process. The agent howled in pain as Angela grabbed his arm and slipped it in an arm bar. Angela snapped the agent's arm and stood back to her feet just as the female agent charged her. Angela stepped out the way landing a quick check hook to the agents chin. She then spun her around in a chokehold using her as a human shield as three more agents barged into the room. Angela pressed her gun into the side of the agents head. "Back the fuck up!" she ordered.

"Drop your weapon now!" one of the agents yelled with his gun trained on the gunman's head.

"Drop your weapons now or else I'll put this bitch brains all over the wall!" Angela threatened. The agents didn't put down their weapons but they did began to slowly back up. She quickly took advantage of the opportunity and shot the three agents down in cold blood. Angela choked the female agent out then gently laid her body down on the floor as she exited the room. Angela snuck out the room and slipped into the staircase just as four more agents stepped off the elevator with their weapons drawn. Angela went down to the basement and exited through a side door. If Mad Max wasn't in his room that meant he was out on the streets somewhere. Being as though Angela found his watch and wallet resting on the nightstand she figured Mad Max couldn't of been prepared for the agents swooping down on him no way he would of left any of his belongings inside that room. *"Perfect,"* Angela said to herself. If Mad Max was out here in the streets not at his best Angela didn't want to miss out on an opportunity like this.

CHAPTER 18

"DEAD MAN RUNNING"

Agent Rebecca stepped out of the water onto the shore and jogged in the direction she heard gunshots coming from. She jogged towards her towel that laid on the beach and removed a silenced 9mm from out of her cooler. Rebecca ran through the streets with a gun in her hand barefoot, she had a murderous look in her eyes. Rebecca crossed the street and saw a small kid standing in the middle of the street kicking a soccer ball. "Hey did you see a man with a gun around here?" she asked in a friendly tone.

The young kid nodded and pointed to a rundown small house. Rebecca slowly made her way to the small house, she reached for the doorknob and found out it was locked. Rebecca took a step back and kicked the front door open. Rebecca stepped inside the house and was greeted with a stiff punch to the side of her face. Mad Max grabbed Rebecca's wrist as the two fought over the gun. Mad Max used his free hand and wrapped it around Rebecca's throat forcing her back to the wall as the gun discharged repeatedly until it was empty. Rebecca landed a hard knee to Mad Max's ribcage but he managed to catch her leg in the process. Mad Max let out an animalistic growl as he lifted Rebecca up over his head and violently slammed her down on her head. Mad Max snatched Rebecca back to her feet by her hair. The agent threw a few punches but Mad Max blocked the blows with ease and delivered a few of his own. Mad

Max stood over Rebecca and stomped her head into the floor repeatedly until Rebecca was no longer moving.

Mad Max walked to the kitchen and grabbed a knife off the knife rack then headed back to the living room where Rebecca laid unconscious. He got ready to stab her when the front door busted open and an agent stood there with a gun aimed at Mad Max's head.

"Drop that knife right this second!" the agent growled as his eyes scanned the entire living room.

"Fuck you!" Mad Max shot back as he flung the knife in the agent's direction and dove out of the way just as the agent pulled the trigger on his weapon. The knife twirled through the air in slow motion before finding a home in the agent's throat. Mad Max walked over, grabbed the agent's gun from off the floor, and put a bullet in the agent's face. Mad Max then walked over to Rebecca and pumped two shots in her chest then made his exit.

***

Later on that night, Mad Max laid on a rundown raggedy looking bed in a low budget hotel staring up at the ceiling. Laying in the tub dead was a woman who he followed from behind and forced his way inside her room. Mad Max needed a place to stay and did what he had to do. Once he got to a phone, he was able to make a phone call and request all the things that he needed be brought to him. Mad Max laid on the bed replaying his entire day in his head. He knew the authorities were getting close to him but he had no clue that they were this close. Mad Max felt stupid for allowing the blonde hair agent to get so close to him in the first place. The ringing of the phone caused Mad Max to snap out of his trance. He rolled over and picked up the phone. "Yeah."

"What the hell happened?" Lieutenant Barkley growled into the receiver. Clearly, he was pissed off.

"A gang of FBI agent swooped down on me while I was on vacation," Mad Max spat. "Why the hell didn't you tell me that they were so close on my ass?"

"I couldn't," Lieutenant Barkley replied. "The entire island is surrounded so please be careful."

"Make the FBI get off my back," Mad Max said. "I need some breathing room so I can make a move."

"Not going to be able to do that," Lieutenant Barkley replied quickly. "You going to have to survive out there for a few days until the heat dies down," he knew that was the last thing Mad Max wanted to hear but he didn't give a shit.

Mad Max shook his head. "What the hell am I going to do here?" he asked with fire in his tone.

"I don't care what you do just don't get arrested," Lieutenant Barkley said. "I'll be in touch!" He said hanging up in Mad Max's ear.

Mad Max hung up the phone when he heard a light knock at the door. He grabbed his gun from under his pillow and made his way to the door. Mad Max looked through the peephole then slowly opened the door. On the other side of the door, a nerdy looking man stood on the other side holding two suitcases in his hand. The scrawny man handed Mad Max the suitcases, nodded then left.

Mad Max laid the suitcases on the bed and opened them. One of the cases were filled with clothes and the second case was filled with weapons. The first thing Mad Max did was take a shower then put on some fresh clothes. He wanted to go out and grab a bite to eat but right now, it was too risky. Several FBI agents had been killed which meant the authorities were out there looking high and low for him. Mad Max sat on the bed watching the news, listening as the reporter spoke on a hotel shootout that also left several agents dead. The more Mad Max listened to the reporter he realized that were adding the bodies in the hotel to his count because the shootout took place in his room. Mad Max cut the

TV off, walked over to the window, and peeked out the blinds. The streets seemed quiet and empty but Mad Max knew better, he knew how sneaky the FBI could be and he also knew that they wouldn't hesitate to kill him on sight.

Mad Max wasn't sure how long he would be able to stay in the hotel room alone before he went crazy.

***

Six days later, Mad Max sat in the same hotel room working out. He did a thousand pushups, then laid on his back and began his sit-ups routine. In the middle of his set, Mad Max heard his phone ringing. He quickly walked over to the phone and answered it. "Yeah."

"Get out of that room now!" Lieutenant Barkley said in an urgent tone.

"Huh? What's going on?" Mad Max asked confused.

"Just get the hell out of that room now!"

Mad Max hung the phone up, walked over towards the window, and peeked through the blinds. His heart sunk down into his stomach when he spotted over fifty S.W.A.T. team member outside the window. "Shit!" Mad Max cursed, as he quickly got dressed. He threw on his black suit, slipped his Kevlar vest on, popped open one of his suitcases, and grabbed a gasmask and slipped it over his head. Max Mad grabbed his M-16 from off the bed and walked back over towards the window. He peeked through the blinds again and saw the S.W.A.T. team getting ready to move in. Without warning, Mad Max took a step back and opened fire through the window taking out several S.W.A.T. members in the process. *"Y'all wanna fuck with me?"* Mad Max said to himself as he watched all the agent's run for cover.

One S.W.A.T. member held up a huge shield and other members took cover behind the shield and returned fire.

Mad Max quickly ducked down as bullets ripped through the window and walls coming from all angles. He stayed in a low crouch in the corner as close to three hundred bullets decorated the walls of the hotel room. The gunfire stopped for a second. Mad Max stayed in his low crouch. Just as he was about to make a move, five cans of tear gas came through the window landing inches away from the assassin. It was a good thing Mad Max had on his gas mask because if he didn't, ain't no telling what the S.W.A.T. team would of done to him. Seconds later, Mad Max watched as several agents slowly climbed through the window. He waited for the perfect time before he sprang from the corner and opened fire on the agents killing them before they even knew what hit them. Mad Max reached over in his suitcase, grabbed a grenade, pulled the pin, and tossed it out the window. When Mad Max heard the loud explosion, he quickly shot to his feet and headed for the front door. He stepped out into the hallway and three shots exploded in the chest area of his vest. Mad Max wasted no time returning fire. Mad Max shot and killed four agents then quickly entered the staircase where two S.W.A.T. agents stood waiting for him. Mad Max walked into the staircase and an agent quickly wrapped a wire around his neck and began to apply pressure while the second agent tried to stab him in the heart with a large hunting knife.

Mad Max grabbed the agents arm blocked the knife strike attempt. He then used the agent's momentum and guided the knife into the neck of the agent who had wrapped the wire around his neck. Mad Max then landed a quick eight-punch combination to agents head then finished him off with a roundhouse kick to the face that sent the agent tumbling down the stairs.

Six more agent sprung around the corner opening fire on the assassin. Mad Max quickly bolted up to the next level and ran out into the hallway. He stopped when he spotted an elderly woman coming out of her room. He quickly tossed the old lady in a chokehold and placed a 9mm to the side of her head. "Don't move!" Mad Max ordered. Two seconds later, the staircase door busted open and the six agents stormed into the hallway.

"Take another step and I'll blow this lady's head off!" Mad Max threatened.

The leader of the pack quickly gunned down the old lady in cold blood. Bullets riddled and rocked the old lady's body killing her on the spot.

"Shit!" Mad Max cursed as a bullet ripped through his thigh as he dove in the old lady's room. He looked up and saw and old man standing there looking at him with a hurt look on his face. Mad Max stood to his feet, roughly grabbed the old man by the collar of his shirt, and shoved him out into the hallway where the agents gunned him down immediately. Mad Max walked to the door, stuck his arm out, and let off nine shots in rapid succession. Mad Max stuck a fresh clip in his gun then pulled out a small mirror and stuck it out the door. He was able to see the agents beginning to make their way towards the room slowly. Mad Max held the mirror at the perfect angle and opened fire hitting all six of his targets. He quickly ran out of the room and shot each agent two more times just to make sure that they were dead. Mad Max picked one of the agent's machine guns and removed the utility belt from around the dead agent's waistline. Two more agents busted through the door and were immediately put down with headshots. Mad Max walked over to the staircase and tossed a can of tear gas inside as several bullets ricochet off the door. From that quick glance, Mad Max could have sworn he'd seen at least forty to fifty S.W.A.T. Agents in the staircase.

CHAPTER 19

"NOWHERE TO RUN"

Captain Spiller pulled up to the scene and stepped out the vehicle with his usual frown on his face. "What the hell is going on?" he asked the head member of the S.W.A.T team.

"We have Mad Max trapped inside the hotel," the head agent said. "We're going to smoke him out one way or another."

"How many men you got on the inside?" Captain Spiller asked curiously.

"Started out with sixty but then I had to call in another forty," the agent replied. "That's a tough son of a bitch in there!"

Captain Spiller spotted Lieutenant Barkley leaning against one of the S.W.A.T. truck looking over a document. "Hey Lieutenant, what are you doing here?"

"Well I got a tip that the suspect was hiding out in this hotel so I made the call," Lieutenant Barkley said. "I'm ready to get rid of this assassin once and for all," he said as the loud sound of machine gun fire could be heard coming from inside the hotel.

"Great work Lieutenant, now all we have to do is wait," Captain Spiller said.

"The S.W.A.T. team shouldn't have an issue taking this guy out," Lieutenant Barkley said with a smirk. If the S.W.A.T. team took Mad Max out he would be a hero and get a promotion, if the S.W.A.T. team failed he'd still be praised for being the only one to be able to pinpoint the assassin's location.

Either way would be a win-win for him. While the two men spoke, a loud explosion could be heard followed by two agents being thrown out a window. Captain Spiller took a few step back as two bodies landed hard on the concrete back to back. Captain Spiller looked up at the window that the agent had been tossed out of and could only imagine what was taking place inside that hotel.

"We're going to need more men in there."

"My men are well trained and are more than capable of handling one man," Lieutenant Barkley said quickly. He secretly wanted the agents to fail so he could continue to do business with Mad Max. "It's only a matter of time before Mad Max is dead."

CHAPTER 20

"NO MORE WAITING"

Angela stood across the street from the hotel with her baseball cap pulled down low and dark shades that helped to hide her true identity. She could hear all the machine gunfire all the way down the block and knew that could only mean one thing. Angela scanned the entire area carefully until she found just what she was looking for. She spotted an agent being carried out of the hotel and placed in the back of an ambulance. Angela quickly made her way over towards the ambulance and entered through the back door. "Nobody move!" she growled with her gun aimed at the EMT workers. "I don't want no trouble, all I want is this agents uniform," Angela said as she began stripping the agent out of his uniform. "Don't be afraid, I'm here to help," Angela said in a polite tone as she slipped in the S.W.A.T. gear. Angela placed the gas mask over her face and exited out the back of the ambulance.

Angela entered the hotel with a two handed grip on her machine gun. *"We have our target trapped in a room on the twelfth floor,"* a voice in her S.W.A.T. earpiece crackled. Angela quickly entered the staircase and began heading up to the twelfth floor. Angela reached the floor she was looking floor and the first thing that caught her attention were the million bullet holes that decorated the entire hallway. Several dead S.W.A.T. members laid dead sprawled out on the floor. The room that Mad Max was in was only about twenty yards away from where she stood. Before Angela got a chance to assess what was going on, she watched as four agents entered the room and immediately the sound of several different guns being fired at the same time could be heard.

***

The first agent barged inside the room and was stunned by a hard kick to the face. Mad Max roughly grabbed the agent pulling him towards him as the other agent ran inside the room and opened fire. The bullets tore down their fellow agent. In the process, Mad Max shot one agent in the face, grabbed the barrel of one of the other agent's gun, and raised it towards the ceiling as the agent kept his finger squeezed down on the trigger. Mad Max kicked the agent in groin when the agent doubled over in pain he shot the agent that stood directly behind him in the face at point blank range. Mad Max then placed the barrel of his gun to the back of the wounded agent's head and pulled the trigger just as two more agents entered the room. The first agent aimed his machine gun at Mad Max's face. Mad Max quickly slapped the gun out of the direction of his face at the same time jerking his head in the opposite direction. Mad Max pulled the agent in close to him and jammed a knife down into the side of the man's neck. Mad Max went to slit the agent's throat when he was hit hard from behind. Mad Max spun around and punched the agent in the nose. The agent took the punch well, then dipped low and picked Mad Max up violently slamming him down to the floor. The agent climbed on top of Mad Max and landed two blows to the assassin's face. Mad Max made it back to his feet and kneed the agent in the ribs then landed an elbow to the side of his face. The agent roughly slung Mad Max into a wall he tried to land a crushing blow to Mad Max's face but he moved his head in the nick of time. The impact from the punch was so strong that his entire arm went through the wall and got stuck. Mad Max jumped up and landed a knee to the agent's elbow snapping it at the joint. Mad Max then crept up on the agent from the behind and violently snapped the man's neck. Mad Max picked up a 9mm from off the floor, spun around, and shot the next two agents that ran through the door. Mad Max reached down, grabbed two grenades off the belt of a dead agent, and made his way to the door. He pulled the pin on one of the grenades and tossed it out into the hallway to keep the rest of the agents at bay. Mad Max then quickly walked over to the middle of the room and pulled the pin on the second grenade and laid it on the middle of the floor then ran and took cover. The explosion was loud and shook the entire building. Mad Max walked back into the middle of the room and saw a gaping hole in the middle of the floor. He quickly removed the uniform of one of the dead agents and slipped it on before jumping through the hole in the floor taking him from the twelfth floor down to the eleventh. Mad Max picked himself up off the floor and jogged out of the room down towards the staircase. He immediately ran into a pack of agents who had their guns trained on him.

"The eleventh floor is clear!" Mad Max announced as the agents let him by, mistaking him for one of their own. Mad max stood with the group of agents for a few minutes before slipping out of sight.

CHAPTER 21

"THE GREAT ESCAPE"

Angela eased her way down the hallway with three agents following her lead. She knew the other agents were no match for the assassin so she decided it was time for her to take a crack at it. Angela tossed a flash grenade inside the room. Two seconds after the explosion, Angela and two other agents quickly entered the room ready to shoot on sight. Angela stood by until she heard the agent in the other room yell out. "Clear!"

Angela looked down at the hole in the floor and knew immediately that Mad Max was trying to escape. She quickly jumped down through the whole landing on the eleventh floor. Angela exited the room and looked for the nearest exit. To her right she spotted the staircase. Angela quickly jogged towards the staircase and busted through the door she ran down the steps skipping two at a time. Angela brushed by an agent exiting the hotel. Angela's eyes scanned the entire area and saw nothing out of the ordinary. "Fuck!" she cursed before discreetly disappearing down an empty street.

***

Mad Max bravely exited the hotel through the front door when another agent bumped into him. From the looks of it, the agent was searching for the assassin but little did he or she know, the assassin was right in front of them. Mad Max walked over towards the ambulance where several EMT workers quickly surrounded him. They offered him water and asked if they could take a look at him since they spotted a gunshot wound to his leg. "I need to go to the hospital," Mad Max said from behind his gas mask. The EMT workers began to work on Mad Max's leg as the ambulance pulled out into the street.

"Sir, do you mind if I take your mask off for a second?" the female worker asked politely.

Mad Max shook his head no, as the EMT worker continued to work on his leg. Once the work on his leg was done, Mad Max sat up.

"Please sir I need you to remain seated," the female told him. "It's for your own safety."

Mad Max replied with a quick chop to the woman's throat. The woman grabbed her throat with two hands as a hard kick to her chest sent her flying through the double doors while the vehicle was still in motion.

"Hey man, what the hell are you doing?" a male EMT worker asked grabbing Mad Max's arm. Mad Max landed a quick three-punch combo to the man's chin knocking him unconscious. When the ambulance slowed down, Mad Max jumped off the back landing on his feet. He then quickly jogged towards the nearest parking lot where he helped himself to the car of his liking.

Mad Max slipped inside the Dodge Charger, hotwired it, and pulled smoothly out of the parking lot. The gunshot wound to his leg was still hurting but at least the female worker had got the bleeding to stop. Now Mad Max had to find a low-key hotel that he could crash at until he could get the proper identification to board a plane. Mad Max drove for over two hours before ditching the stolen car. He then took a cab forty-five minutes further out to a decent looking hotel. Mad Max walked into the hotel, purchased a hat from the gift shop, and pulled the brim down low so it could keep his identity safe from the security cameras that were posted up all around the hotel. Once he had his room key, Mad Max hurried up to his room so he could tend to all of his injuries. He busted inside the bathroom and grabbed the first aid kit that rested under the sink. The first thing he did was remove the bandage from his leg. Mad Max winced in pain as he began to stitch himself up. Throughout the years, Mad Max learned how to take care of and repair his body for times like this. In his line of work, going to the hospital when you're injured was like asking to be thrown in jail for the rest of your life and something he refused to do under no circumstances. Mad Max limped back over towards his bed, took a few pain pills, and shut his eyes. He and his body could really use the rest. Mad Max wasn't a religious man but he was thankful to be alive and even more thankful to have gotten away with his freedom. Mad Max laid his 9mm on the bed within arm's reach then finally drifted off to sleep. He needed as much rest as he could get because tomorrow he had a big day ahead of him.

CHAPTER 22

"WHAT NOW?"

Angela sat on the plane with her face buried in her laptop. She was upset that Mad Max was able to slip through the cracks again but she refused to let that get her down. The plane she sat on was headed to Paris. She knew the only way she was going to find Mad Max was to find his girl, Samantha Hancock first. Angela knew if she found Samantha finding Mad Max wouldn't be far behind. On her computer, Angela was doing all the research she could find on Samantha. From all the research she'd done, Angela discovered that Samantha worked for the C.I.A. doing I.T. work. Angela knew if she followed Samantha, she would lead her straight to Mad Max. Angela got up and walked to the back of the plane towards the restroom when she noticed what looked like an undercover agent sitting at the back of plane watching her like a hawk. The difference between Angela and a regular person was Angela knew exactly what to look for when pinpointing who was who and the man that sat at the back of the plane definitely stood out like a sore thumb. Everything about the man screamed agent and officer. Angela used the restroom then looked at herself in the mirror for a second. She now had to figure out how to shake the agent and hope there wouldn't be a gang of other officers and agents waiting to pick her up when the plane landed in Paris. Angela made it back to her seat, closed her laptop, and prepared for the plane to land. Angela grabbed a pencil and slipped it down in her pocket as the plane began preparing for landing. Twenty-five minutes later, the plane finally came to a stop and all the passengers stood and began getting their bags from the bins up above. Angela pretended to be busy but really she was focused and kept a close eye on the agent without him realizing it.

"Have a nice day," Angela said politely to the stewardess as she stepped off the plane. Angela walked through the airport and made several quick pit stops at a few gift shops just to see if the agent was really following her. Just as she figured, every time Angela made a stop, so did the agent. This gave Angela confirmation that she had to kill the agent if she wanted to keep her freedom. Angela slipped off into the ladies room and saw three other women washing their hands at the sink.

"Sorry ladies y'all have to go," Angela said forcefully shoving the woman out the restroom.

Once the restroom was empty, Angela placed her back up against the wall, pulled the pencil that she had taken from the plane, and gripped it in the palm of her hand. She waited for a few seconds and remained quiet as she watched the bathroom door ease open. The agent stepped in the restroom and Angela quickly sprung off the wall and jammed the pencil in the agent's neck. Out of instincts, the agent grabbed Angela's wrist as the two struggled in the restroom. The agent landed a punch to Angela's stomach, forcing her back into the wall. Angela responded with a knee to the agent's rib cage and slipped out of the agent's grasp.

The agent frowned as he removed the pencil out of his neck and tossed it down to the floor and charged Angela. Angela sidestepped the agent's movement and landed an upper cut to the agent's chin. A four-punch combo followed leaving the agent on wobbly legs. The agent went to grapple Angela and was rewarded with a knee to the face.

Angela easily took the agent down to the floor and put her foot on his chest. "Why are you following me?" Angela asked with a stone look on her face.

"I need an ambulance," the agent growled with his hand held up to his neck.

Angela applied more pressure to the agent's chest. "Last time I'm going to ask you," she warned.

"Fuck you!" the agent growled. "You're a disgrace," he said as he spat in Angela's direction.

Angela moved her foot from the agent's chest up to his neck and applied major pressure. She watched as the agent squirmed around on the floor gasping for air. His legs moved like a fish out of water until finally they stopped moving completely. Angela quickly searched through the dead agent's pockets. While she was fishing through the dead man's pockets, the bathroom door busted open and a heavyset woman walked in and stopped dead in his tracks. Angela picked the bloody pencil up off the floor and charged the big woman forcefully backing her up into the wall. "Close your fucking eyes!" Angela growled as she stuck the pencil up under the big woman's neck.

"Please don't kill me," the big man begged. Angela removed the big man's belt from his waist, tied the man's hands behind his back, and made him get on his knees.

"If you scream I promise I'll blow your head off!" Angela growled in the big man's ear. "Stay here and don't move!" Angela said as she exited the restroom. Angela walked out of the restroom and power walked as fast as she could without looking suspicious.

Outside the airport, Angela jumped in a cab and headed straight for Samantha's job. Angela knew that the only way to get to Mad Max was through Samantha, she was tired the hiding seek games it was time to get her revenge once and for all.

CHAPTER 23

"WRONG PLACE AT THE WRONG TIME"

Samantha stepped off the elevator that led to the underground garage. She was dressed in a gray suit, her hair was pulled back into a ponytail, the look on her face screamed aggravated. Samantha walked through the garage until she reached her Audi. Samantha got behind the wheel of her car, backed out of her parking spot, and exited the garage. Samantha sang along with the radio when she felt something sharp pinching the side of her neck.

"Keep driving and don't make any sudden moves," Angela whispered from the back seat as she held a pocketknife that she'd purchased from the hardware store to Samantha's neck.

"Who the hell are you?" Samantha tried to remain cool but her voice gave away her nervousness.

"I'm your worst nightmare," Angela growled.

"What do you want?" Samantha asked.

"I want your boyfriend," Angela replied. "Where can I find Mad Max?"

"How would I know?"

Angela dug the tip of the knife a little further into Samantha's neck to the point it drew blood. "I will kill you right here in this car if you keep playing with me!"

"I haven't seen Mad Max in years," Samantha lied as she pulled into the garage of her home.

Angela exited the car and roughly snatched Samantha out the driver's seat by the back of her collar. "Open the door now!"

Samantha fumbled around in her purse before finally finding her house keys. Once inside the house, Angela spun Samantha around and landed a solid blow to her chin knocking her unconscious. While Samantha was knocked out, Angela took it upon herself to search the house to make sure that the two of them were alone. Angela searched under Samantha's pillow and found a machine gun with an extended clip. A smile danced on Angela's lips she knew that Samantha was indeed the girlfriend of an assassin. What other type of woman would sleep with a machine gun under their pillow?

Angela made it back downstairs and splashed some water on Samantha's face in an attempt to wake her up but it didn't work. "Wake up!" Angela said as she gave Samantha's face a couple of slaps until she finally came around.

"Where am I?" Samantha said in a drowsy tone. She frantically looked around as if she didn't recognize her own home.

"Tell me where I can find Mad Max," Angela said looking Samantha dead in her eyes.

"If I tell you anything, he'll kill me," Samantha pleaded.

"And what the fuck do you think I'm going to do to you if you don't tell me what I want to hear?" Angela asked with a stone look on her face. If Samantha refused to tell Angela what she wanted to hear Angela was willing to beat it out of her if she had to. "Last time I'm going to ask you."

"Please don't do this," Samantha pleaded as tears rolled down her cheeks.

Angela turned and slapped the taste out of Samantha's mouth then violently pulled her to her feet by her hair and tossed her into the wall. "You sure this how you wanna do this?" Angela asked as she went low landing a strong hook Samantha's stomach.

Samantha doubled over in pain, and then dropped to one knee. She spit up half of her lunch.

"Still ain't got nothing to say?" Angela asked as she lifted her leg and kicked Samantha in the face sending her crashing into the living room.

"Please stop!" Samantha begged with blood running from her nose and mouth. "I have money; it's yours you can take all of it!" She sobbed with her hands up in surrender.

Angela grabbed Samantha's pinky finger and snapped it like a twig.

"Arrrrrrgh!" Samantha howled rolling around on the floor in tremendous pain. Angela walked over to the kitchen, removed a sharp knife from off the rack, and headed towards Samantha.

"You must really love Mad Max," Angela said as her eyes went from Samantha down to the knife she held in her hand. "You sure this the route you wanna go?" she asked. "You better start talking!"

"Please don't do this," Samantha cried as she looked at the sharp knife in the Teflon Queen's hand. "Mad Max doesn't tell me anything."

Without warning, Angela sliced Samantha on the palm of her hand.

Samantha cried as the knife sliced her hand, then her arm, then her chest. Angela got ready to stab Samantha in her stomach when she yelled out. "Okay, okay, I'll tell you!"

"Start talking," Angela stood over Samantha in an intimidating fashion. The look on her face told Samantha that this was in fact her last chance.

"Mad Max is on his way back from Jamaica," Samantha cried holding her bloody hand. "I'm supposed to book a hotel and meet him there later on tonight," she confessed.

"How do I know you're not lying to me?" Angela asked with a raised brow. "You wouldn't lie to me now would you?"

"I've told you everything and now it's only a matter of time before they find my body floating in a river somewhere," Samantha said in a disgusting tone. Snitching went against everything that she believed in but when it came to taking pain Samantha wasn't the one.

"I'm going to kill Mad Max so now no one will be dumping your body in the river," Angela said.

Samantha laughed and shook her head. "You agents are dumber than I thought," she chuckled. "You think me and Mad Max pulled all this off on our own?"

"Y'all had more help?"

"Of course," Samantha said as she wrapped her bloody hand in a dishrag to try and stop the bleeding. "Lieutenant Barkley is the one who put this whole little plan into play,"

"Lieutenant Barkley?" Angela repeated as she hit the record button on her phone to make sure she was hearing everything correctly.

"Yes he was the mastermind behind this entire plan," Samantha said. "He paid me a handsome fee to get the information he needed then had Mad Max steal it for him."

"So why would Lieutenant Barkley want other agents dead?" Angela asked confused. None of this was making sense to her.

"More dead agents meant more leverage," Samantha said. "He was going to have Mad Max be the face to what he planned, then when it was time to agree to the demands he said he would be the person to okay Mad Max's offer then in the end us three would split all the profit."

"I never trusted that motherfucker," Angela said.

"I never trusted him either," Samantha, said quickly. "I didn't agree with the plan from the jump but Mad Max convinced me that he could pull the plan off so me like a dumbass went along with it."

"It's okay we all make mistakes," Angela said in an attempt to make Samantha feel better. Angela walked over to the counter, grabbed the cordless phone, and handed it to Samantha. "Here, call Mad Max and confirm the meeting time and place."

Samantha dialed a few numbers on the phone then place it up to her ear. "Hey baby where you at?"

"Just got off the plane," Mad Max replied. "You at the spot already?"

"No, I'm about to leave now I just wanted to make sure your plane landed on time," Samantha lied in her usual bubbly voice hoping that Mad Max didn't sense that something was off.

"I'll be there in an hour," Mad Max said. "And have some food waiting for me and wear something sexy."

"Anything for you daddy," Samantha purred. "See you soon."

"Good job," Angela said removing the phone from her hand and sitting it back on the charger. "Come on we have to go." Angela helped clean the blood off of Samantha's face and made her put on long sleeves to hide the fresh cuts on her arms.

CHAPTER 24

"NO TURNING BACK"

amantha pulled up in front of the hotel. She and Angela stepped out and entered the hotel leaving the valet worker to park the Audi. Samantha walked up to the front desk received her room key and headed towards the elevator. "So?" Samantha said.

"So what?"

"Are you going to kill him?" Samantha asked as her eyes began to water. The elevator doors opened and Angela quickly stepped on the elevator making sure she ignored Samantha's question. "Can you do it quickly please," Samantha said as tears began to run down her face.

Angela nodded.

"Can't you just arrest him instead of killing him?" Samantha asked.

"It's a little too late for all that now," Angela, said as the elevator dinged and the doors opened. The two women stepped off the elevator and headed down the hall until they reached the room they were looking for. Samantha slipped her card in the slot, the lock on the door flashed green then the two women let themselves inside the room. Once inside the room, Angela pulled her 9mm from the small of her back and attached a silencer on the barrel.

"So this is it huh?" Samantha said. Tears still streaming down her face.

"Don't start that shit!" Angela barked. "Suck it up and glad you ain't going to the same place he is."

"But I love him," Samantha pleaded. A part of her felt bad for setting her man up and wish she could take it back but at the time the pain was unbearable.

Angela aimed her weapon at Samantha's face. "One more peep out of you and I'm going to shoot you in the face," she warned causing Samantha to hush her mouth. Angela called herself looking out for Samantha by not killing her but now she was giving that option a second thought. Angela sat on the window seal and waited patiently.

***

Mad Max's cab came to a stop directly in front of the hotel; he paid the driver and slipped out the back seat dressed in an expensive navy blue suit. Mad Max walked through the lobby with the confidence of a lion amongst a bunch of sheep. He boarded the elevator and stood with his back facing the wall. Mad Max was glad to still be alive and even more grateful that he would be inactive for a while; it was time for him to start spending more time with Samantha. She deserved way more time than he was giving her and he now planned to make that up to her. Mad Max stepped off the elevator and made his way down the hall. Mad Max stopped in front of the door he was looking for and lightly knocked on the door. From the other side of the door Samantha's voice replied.

"It's open."

Mad Max grabbed the doorknob and pushed forward.

CHAPTER 25

"IT IS WHAT IT IS"

Angela sat on the window seal when she heard a light knock at the door. She quickly shot to her feet with a two handed grip on her weapon and a serious look on her face. She looked over at Samantha and nodded her head towards the door.

"It's open," Samantha said loud of enough for Mad Max to hear it from the other side of the door. The doorknob turned and door slowly began to open.

Angela stood with her arms locked at the elbow ready to shoot whoever walked through the front door. Just as the door opened, Mad Max stepped inside the room with a smile on his face. His smile quickly disappeared when he saw Angela standing there with a pistol aimed at his face.

"Nooooo!" Samantha yelled as she ran and pushed Mad Max out of the line of fire just as Angela pulled the trigger. The bullet hit Samantha in the back of her neck as her and Mad Max stumbled out the room. Mad Max quickly tossed Samantha's dead body to the floor and took off in a sprint down the hall.

Angela stepped over Samantha's body and took off after Mad Max. Mad Max didn't have a gun on him so all he could do was run. He quickly dashed inside the staircase and ran up towards the roof. Mad Max reached the roof and looked around for another exit. "Fuck!" he cursed after looking around and realizing the only way off the roof was to go over the side. Mad Max hid behind the door just as Angela was coming through it. Mad Max kicked Angela's wrist sending the gun flying in the air. Angela wasted no time and threw a five-punch combination at Mad Max. He blocked most of the blows, picked Angela up, and slammed her down on the small pebbles that covered the roof. Angela hit the ground hard wrapped her hand around Mad Max's throat and tried to choke the life out of him. Mad Max punched Angela on the side of her head just as she flipped him over her head. They both quickly shot to their feet and froze when the door leading to the roof busted open and several FBI agents flooded the roof as a downpour of rain came out of nowhere.

"Both of y'all on the ground now!" one of the FBI agents yelled. Neither Angela nor Mad Max budged. Seconds later, Captain Spiller busted through the door followed by Lieutenant Barkley, Troy, and Ashley.

"Everyone lower your weapons now!" Captain Spiller ordered. He then looked out towards Angela and gave her a head nod followed by a wink.

Angela returned Captain Spiller's wink and slowly walked towards Mad Max. She took a fighting stance once the two were within striking distance all the agents surrounded the two assassins forming a make-believe ring as the rain came down even harder. Angela let out an animalistic growl as her and Mad Max went at each other hard. Each assassin tried to kill the one that stood before the other. Angela blocked several blows with her hands and elbows. Angela waited for the perfect opportunity and attempted a flying knee that hit Mad Max in the forehead. Angela threw a strong kick that Mad Max ducked but she followed up in the same motion and landed a roundhouse to the side of Mad Max's head. Mad Max caught Angela's leg in the process and swept her other leg from under her. Mad Max stomped Angela's head into the wet gravel and followed up with several hard kicks to her ribs and stomach area. Mad Max roughly grabbed Angela up to her feet by her hair and landed three strong blows to her face. Rain splashed off Angela's face with each punch delivered to her face.

"Get him Angela!" Ashley cheered Angela on from the sideline as she watched her mentor taking a beating.

Mad Max dragged Angela across the rough gravel by her hair. "I'm about to toss this bitch off the roof!" Mad Max announced with a sickening smile on his face. Mad Max grabbed Angela and lifted her over his head. As he went to toss Angela off the roof, she somehow manage slip out of his grasp and slid behind Mad Max. Angela went to shove Mad Max off the roof and in the process he managed to grab her and they both went flying off the roof.

CHAPTER 26

"END ALL BE ALL"

"Nooooooo!" Ashley screamed as she and Captain Spiller ran towards the edge of the roof. They couldn't believe what they just saw. With all the rain coming down along with the tears in Ashley's eyes made it even harder for her to see. Ashely reached the edge and looked down only to see both Angela and Mad Max hanging on to the ledge with one hand.

Mad Max kicked Angela in the ribs while hanging on with one hand. He went to kick Angela again but this time she caught his leg with her free hand and gave his leg a strong tug. That strong tug was all it took for Mad Max to lose his grip on the wet ledge. Mad Max fell but grabbed on to Angela's ankle and held on for dear life.

"Please help me!" Mad Max said looking up in Angela's eyes.

"I hope you burn in hell!" Angela growled as she raised her free leg and kicked Mad Max in the face forcing him to release his grip on her ankle. Angela watched as Mad Max fell to his death.

Captain Spiller and Ashley quickly helped pull Angela back up on the roof where she laid on her back with her eyes closed.

"Out of the way!" Lieutenant Barkley barked. "Arrest her!" he ordered.

Ashley looked on with a hurt look on her face as the FBI agents arrested her mentor.

"Hold it right there!" Troy yelled grabbing everyone's attention. He pulled out his phone and play the playback of Samantha talking about the part that Lieutenant Barkley placed in the entire master plan. Angela had forwarded the audio to Troy for insurance purposes and it paid off.

"Arrest him!" Captain Spiller growled as he watched the FBI agents roughly slam Lieutenant Barkley down on the hard wet pebbles and cuff.

"You can't do this to me!" Lieutenant Barkley yelled. "I've served my country for years!"

"Get this scumbag out of my sight," Captain Spiller said with a disgusted look on his face. Ashley walked over and uncuffed Angela.

"I'm sorry for all the stuff you had to go through," Ashley apologized as if it was all her fault.

Angela flashed a weak smile. "It's not your fault sweetie," she looked over at Troy and gave him a hug. "Thank you," she whispered in his ear.

"We family," Troy reminded her.

Angela made her way over to Captain Spiller and hugged him tightly. "Thank you for believing in me and trying to help me," she flashed a bloody smile.

For once, Captain Spiller cracked a smile. "You had me worried there for a second," he said honestly.

"I'm getting old, Captain," Angela gave him a wink and began to walk off.

"Hey you know we can always use another agent," Captain Spiller called out. "What do you say?"

"I'm done, Captain. There's a new sheriff in town," Angela nodded towards Ashley. With that being said, she limped towards the exit without saying another word.

"You think she'll be back?" Troy asked.

Ashley looked as Angela limped away. "I wish I could answer that."

THE END

BOOKS BY GOOD2GO AUTHORS

GOOD 2 GO FILMS PRESENTS

**THE HAND I WAS DEALT- FREE WEB SERIES
NOW AVAILABLE ON YOUTUBE!
YOUTUBE.COM/SILKWHITE212**

SEASON TWO NOW AVAILABLE

To order books, please fill out the order form below:

To order films please go to www.good2gofilms.com

Name:_____

Address:_____

City: _____ State: _____ Zip Code: _____

Phone:_____

Email:_____

Method of Payment: Check   VISA   MASTERCARD

Credit Card#:_____

Name as it appears on card: _____

Signature: _____

Item Name	Price	Qty	Amount
48 Hours to Die – Silk White	$14.99		
Business Is Business – Silk White	$14.99		
Business Is Business 2 – Silk White	$14.99		
Business Is Business 3 – Silk White	$14.99		
Childhood Sweethearts – Jacob Spears	$14.99		
Childhood Sweethearts 2 – Jacob Spears	$14.99		
Childhood Sweethearts 3 - Jacob Spears	$14.99		
Flipping Numbers – Ernest Morris	$14.99		
Flipping Numbers 2 – Ernest Morris	$14.99		
He Loves Me, He Loves You Not - Mychea	$14.99		
He Loves Me, He Loves You Not 2 - Mychea	$14.99		
He Loves Me, He Loves You Not 3 - Mychea	$14.99		
He Loves Me, He Loves You Not 4 – Mychea	$14.99		
He Loves Me, He Loves You Not 5 – Mychea	$14.99		
Lost and Turned Out – Ernest Morris	$14.99		
Married To Da Streets – Silk White	$14.99		
M.E.R.C. - Make Every Rep Count Health and Fitness	$14.99		
My Besties – Asia Hill	$14.99		
My Besties 2 – Asia Hill	$14.99		
My Besties 3 – Asia Hill	$14.99		
My Besties 4 – Asia Hill	$14.99		
My Boyfriend's Wife - Mychea	$14.99		
My Boyfriend's Wife 2 – Mychea	$14.99		
Never Be The Same – Silk White	$14.99		
Stranded – Silk White	$14.99		
Slumped – Jason Brent	$14.99		
Tears of a Hustler - Silk White	$14.99		
Tears of a Hustler 2 - Silk White	$14.99		
Tears of a Hustler 3 - Silk White	$14.99		
Tears of a Hustler 4- Silk White	$14.99		
Tears of a Hustler 5 – Silk White	$14.99		
Tears of a Hustler 6 – Silk White	$14.99		
The Panty Ripper - Reality Way	$14.99		

The Panty Ripper 3 – Reality Way	$14.99		
The Teflon Queen – Silk White	$14.99		
The Teflon Queen 2 – Silk White	$14.99		
The Teflon Queen 3 – Silk White	$14.99		
The Teflon Queen 4 – Silk White	$14.99		
The Teflon Queen 5 – Silk White	$14.99		
The Teflon Queen 6 - Silk White	$14.99		
Tied To A Boss - J.L. Rose	$14.99		
Tied To A Boss 2 - J.L. Rose	$14.99		
Time Is Money - Silk White	$14.99		
Young Goonz – Reality Way	$14.99		
Subtotal:			
Tax:			
Shipping (Free) U.S. Media Mail:			
Total:			

Make Checks Payable To:
Good2Go Publishing
7311 W Glass Lane,
Laveen, AZ 85339

CPSIA information can be obtained
at www.ICGtesting.com
Printed in the USA
LVOW04s1737021216
515533LV00009B/552/P